AFTER H

To Sarah, lots of love, Pam xxx

PAM BLOOM PUBLISHING

PAM BLOOM

After Harry
Copyright © Pam Bloom

Published by Pam Bloom Publishing

All rights reserved. No part of this publication may be reproduced, distributed, or transmitted in any form or by any means, including photocopying, recording, or other electronic or mechanical methods, without the prior written permission of the publisher, except in the case of brief quotations embodied in critical reviews and certain other non-commercial uses permitted by copyright law.

ISBN: 978-0-9955272-5-6

Cover design by Ilan Sheady,
Unclefrankproductions.com

Author's note: This book was written and produced in the UK, and uses British English language conventions.

Also by Pam Bloom:

Whole New World[s]
Running
(Books 1 and 2 of The Parallel Universe Adventures)

Connect with Pam at her website,
www.pambloomauthor.com

Dedicated to everyone with an open mind

Chapter 1

The trees started screaming the day after Harry died. They didn't stop for three days, by which time I was certain I had gone totally mad.

Harry was...

Oh, Harry... darling, dear, sweet little Harry. My innocent little angel. My love, my life. My everything.

Harry was... my only child, a longed-for and long planned-for son. Late arriving – I was 36 – he was my hope for the future. My reason to get up in the morning. My reason to live.

And then one day he was gone, just like that. Snap.

One minute he was there, trundling along on his Batman scooter, merrily making his way ten steps in front of me to pre-school. Me lugging his lunchbox and coat – it was a sunny day in March, and he'd been too hot to wear it, but I knew it was going to rain later so insisted he take it along. I was huffing and puffing, impatient, knowing if we didn't get a move on I'd miss my bus to work.

He was happy as a sandboy, as usual, singing some song off the telly to himself as he scooted along...

...and then...

And then...

Sorry, even now I find it hard to put into words just what happened.

The car that hit him was white... I remember seeing it shining in the sun as it flashed in front of me. I don't think Harry even knew he was on the road. I mean, we'd been doing all the usual 'stop at the kerb' things, and the 'look both ways' thing, and the 'wait for the green man' thing at crossings, but... well, Harry was only three, and there were too many other things in his head to worry about stopping at kerbs.

I'm sure I shouted at him to stop, just before he scooted out into the road... I don't remember it very clearly, thankfully. I think my brain's blotted it out, somehow. Well, I know it has, because of the trees. The trees took over, after.

Then... then he was gone. Just like that.

The day after, the trees started screaming.

I woke in a haze of sedative, fuzzy, not knowing where I was or why I was there. Head hurting badly. One moment of fuzziness, then the recollection of Harry's death hit me like a white car. My angel was dead.

I tried, briefly, to recall the day before, but couldn't remember anything after it happened; the shock had sent me into oblivion.

I couldn't think, or feel, or see, or smell. All I could hear was screaming. High pitched, incessant, screaming, like a stuck record – remember them? The needle had got stuck, and the screaming went on and on, the same tone, the same sound, just over and over and over...

Dimly, slowly, like emerging out of a nightmare, I heard other noises around me. Voices, low and concerned. Buzzing, like a chainsaw. A news programme on the radio. My mum's voice, choked. My sister's voice, soothing. Another I didn't recognise.

I opened my eyes and saw a familiar room. My bedroom. So I was at home, in bed. The voices were coming from just outside the door, but I couldn't hear what they were saying, just mumbles. I could smell bacon frying.

I closed my eyes again and cried myself silently back into the fog of forgetfulness.

When I awoke once more the world was brighter. Sun was shining through the window, but the curtains were still shut.

There was someone sitting on the bottom of my bed.

I looked at them, uncomprehending. The screaming was still there. I thought it must be my brain, rebelling at the thought of my baby dying, and was not really concerned. After all, nothing mattered any more. But I thought I'd better check, anyhow.

The man at the bottom of the bed smiled at me and put a hand on my arm, which was resting outside the covers. My hand looked like it belonged to somebody else.

The man was dark, about 40, I supposed, and had a kind face.

"Hello," he said, and without waiting for me to reply, "I'm Dr Reed. You may feel a bit disorientated for a while, because I've been sedating you, but I'm sure you'll begin to feel better soon."

Yeah, right, I thought, like I'm ever going to feel better ever again – don't you know Harry's dead? But I said: "Can you hear screaming?" My voice sounded thin and tiny and scratched.

The doctor frowned. He shook his head. "No," he said gently, patting my arm again. "That's the chainsaws outside. They're cutting the trees down, remember?"

Get your patronising hand off me, I thought. Harry's dead, and you think patting my arm will make me feel better? But I said: "Oh, it must be the trees screaming, then," and shut my eyes again. Oblivion took a while this time, but I went there in the end. I welcomed it.

The next time I woke there was no-one else in the room. It was dim, like that light you get just before evening. My stomach made a grumbling noise, as if it was hungry. I didn't remember when I'd last eaten, but again this didn't matter. Harry was dead, and I didn't care if I never ate again.

The trees were fainter now, as if they were going away.

I listened hard, but couldn't hear anything else.

Not wanting to get out of bed again, ever – I just wanted to lie there and die, to go wherever Harry had gone – I closed my eyes again and waited. But this time sleep didn't come. I supposed the sedatives must have eventually worn off.

After a while – five minutes, an hour, I've no idea – I decided I'd just go and ask the doctor to give me some more, so I swung my feet over the side of the bed and pushed the duvet back. The carpet felt hard under my feet – it was a cheap one I'd bought the year before, after Harry's dad left, and I'd never really liked it – and I felt for my slippers, which were under the bed as usual.

As I stood, a bit shaky, I dimly noticed I was wearing pyjamas. I always slept naked, and didn't even know I **had** a pair of pyjamas. These were a bit big, and a cheery red colour. I wondered whose they were, but wasn't really interested. Harry was dead, and what did it matter what I wore anyway?

I put the slippers on and shuffled to the door. On the way I glanced at the full-length mirror on the wardrobe to my left, and saw a crooked, old lady with wild hair and dead eyes. I supposed it was me.

I opened the door and stood on the landing, listening. To the right was the bathroom, door open, empty, and to the left a closed door with a ceramic sign showing a green cartoon tractor being ridden by a ruddy-faced cartoon farmer. The sign said 'Harry's room,' but I really didn't want to go there right now. Not now.

I shuffled across the landing, legs feeling like jelly, and made my way to the top of the stairs. There were sounds coming from downstairs, muffled, but I couldn't tell if it was the TV or someone speaking. In the background, dimly now, the trees were still crying out in pain.

As I placed my foot on the first step, a door was opened downstairs and my sister's voice said: "Steph? Is that you?"

No, I thought, it's a ghost. Who else would it be?

I put another foot on the stair, and nearly fell headlong. My slipper slipped and I twisted my ankle as I brought it down, clutching at the bannister with a clawed hand. So my body still wanted to live, anyway, I thought briefly, as I sat down heavily on the second step.

Andrea was by now hurrying up the stairs towards me, face bleak and scared. She hadn't done her hair, I noticed, but was still immaculately turned out, though her make-up was a little streaked from tears.

"Oh my God, Steph, what are you doing out of bed?" she asked. "The doctor said you should get complete bed rest. Come on, let's get you back up."

She pulled me up and tried to lead me upstairs again, but I turned back and, without saying a word, continued downstairs.

"Oh... oh... OK," she said, still holding my arm. "Come on, then, let's go and make you a cup of tea."

Together we made it down and into the kitchen, where I fell rather than sat onto a chair. Andrea filled up the kettle and started making tea, chattering away all the while. I've no idea what she was saying, it was obviously just to fill the silence.

I looked around at the neat little kitchen, Harry's scribblings stuck with magnets to the fridge – one showed me and him, apparently, though it looked more like a giraffe and a tiger – a pile of washed dishes on the drainer, Harry's school coat on a peg by the back door. He'll never wear that again, I thought, and started crying silently, tears falling onto the unfamiliar pyjamas.

*Oh no, what do I do now? What do I say? What **can** I say? How on earth do you cope with losing your only child? And so young? Why did this happen? Why, God, why?*

It was Andrea's voice, but in a kind of distant way, as though she were talking with her hand in front of her mouth. I stared up at her, and saw her looking at me, kettle in hand, concerned look on her face. Her mouth wasn't moving. She wasn't saying a word. But I could still hear her.
Why? Why? Why, God, why?
The trees were still screaming.
Why?

Chapter 2

Andrea stood in front of me, watching me carefully. "Tea or coffee?" she asked – and this time her mouth moved when the words came out.

I was so confused and fuzzy in the head that I said nothing, so she sort of shrugged and said: "Tea it is, then!" in a false bright way, as if she was talking to her favourite vicar.

Three years my senior, Andrea was – still is – a staunch Christian. One of those who's constantly going on about it, as if there's no doubt about the facts of God's love and Jesus's continued existence in a vague but undeniable heaven, and anyone who thinks otherwise is a complete idiot who deserves to suffer.

I myself believe in nothing I can't see proven – **you** can believe what you like, I don't care, as long as you don't persecute anyone else because they don't believe in the same god as you.

I always, even as a child, found Andrea's extreme religious views irritating. In the last few years, however, she'd become even worse in her evangelising. When Gerry and I got married in the local register office she went spare. When I refused to get Harry christened, she didn't speak to me for two weeks. And when she did it was to go on about what would happen to Harry's soul if he should die.

Well, now I suppose she thought he was in limbo, or hell or something. Let her. I knew where he was.

She made the tea and put it down in front of me before sitting opposite at the table, red eyes pitying. She was saying something about being glad to see me awake and hoping I'd be feeling better soon, and I wanted to reply but couldn't seem to find my voice.

Then I remembered what I had come down here for. "Where's the doctor?" I asked.

Andrea stopped prattling on and started a little. "Dr Reed?" she said.

I remembered the man at the bottom of the bed, and nodded slowly.

She looked puzzled. "He's not here anymore," she said gently. "He had to go. But he left you some pills in case you feel you can't cope."

And she got up, went over to the worktop and came back with a packet of pills, which she put in front of me on the table.

"I think you can take four a day or something – the instructions are inside. He said they'd make it a bit more bearable for you."

Idly, I picked the pills up and turned them over in my hand. "Will they make me go to sleep?" I asked. My voice still sounded distant, like it was coming from someone else.

Andrea shook her head. "They're..." *anti-depressants...* "to make you feel better," she said. I heard the word in the middle of that sentence, but her lips didn't make it.

I put the pills down. If they weren't going to bring oblivion, I wasn't interested.

"Try and drink your tea," she said, pushing the mug towards me. "You must be dehydrated, you haven't had anything to eat or drink since..." *Harry died. Oh, God, you look terrible, sis. Please get a grip.*

"I can't," I said. "I...I can't..." my voice tailed off, and suddenly Andrea got up, came over to me and hugged me tight, her tears dripping onto my shoulder.

We sat there, crying, for what seemed like hours. All the time I could hear her voice, mumbling, incoherent some of the time, clear at other times, but she was not saying a word, just sobbing; and it dawned on me that I was listening to her thoughts. Actually able to hear her thinking. It interested me in a distracted sort of way. At one point she was thinking about Harry, and how sweet he had been to her last time they met.

Sweet, innocent little boy her thoughts went. *Dear, sweet little Harry...* and then: *How sad he'll never know the love of God. How selfish of Steph not to think of his soul.*

I pulled away from her. Even in her innermost thoughts she was criticising me, just like she had done since I was a baby.

She looked down at me, still sitting in the chair, and wiped her eyes with her sleeve.

I said nothing.

She sat down again, and patted my hand on the table. "I don't want you to worry about anything," she said, sniffling. "We've made all the arrangements already. You just have to concentrate on getting better."

I didn't understand at first, but then she went on: "Reverend Cooper is really happy to do the service. We booked it for next Friday – we were really lucky to get the church, as he's very busy at the moment. He said you ought to pick the hymns and let him know what readings you want, but I said you'd probably let **me** do that, as I know them better than you, and..."

I couldn't believe this. "What on **earth** are you talking about, Andrea?" I yelled. Well, at least my voice has returned, I thought.

She looked shocked, but suitably ashamed, too, I believe. "What... what do you mean?" she asked quietly.

"How **dare** you go behind my back and arrange my son's funeral without even asking?" I stormed, angrier than I had ever been at her.

Her face changed to defensive. "You were in no fit state," she said. "You've been comatose since it happened, and the funeral directors said we needed to start the arrangements as soon as possible, and Gerry said he didn't care what form it took, and..."

"And you thought you'd give poor old Harry a Christian send-off so your God would take pity on him and let him into the kingdom, is that it?" I asked, calmer now I'd regained my voice.

She wrinkled her forehead in the way she always did when she was being told off.

"Well... yes," she said. "I didn't think you'd mind."

"Mind? Of course I mind. This is the last thing I'm going to do for my only child, and God is not even going to get a look-in, thank you very much.

"There'll be no church, no hymns, no readings and no bloody prayers, either. None of those things meant anything to Harry, and they certainly don't mean anything to me."

Andrea was now rubbing her head as if it was hurting her. "But Reverend Cooper..." she started.

"Tell him to go fuck himself," I said, picking up my mug of tea and taking a sip. It tasted sweet. I hated sugar in tea, and Andrea knew it.

Oh dear Lord, please open up her mind and soul to thy goodness and mercy, and let her...

I could hear her, clear as day, though her mouth was now fixed in a tight little smile that was part nerves and part upset.

"And you can stop praying for me, too," I said, getting up shakily to make myself a new cup of tea.

Chapter 3

For the next couple of days I seemed to exist in a constant fog of torment. Everything, from dressing to eating, speaking to even thinking, seemed pointless and took so much effort.

I had loads of visitors, of course – you always see plenty of people in the few days after a death, as family and friends get to hear the bad news and come to pay their respects and see how you're doing. Most of them even care.

But I didn't want any visitors. Not Aunt Sarah, who I hadn't seen for six years and hadn't even been sure she was still alive when I last sent her a Christmas card. Not my best friend Jenny, kind Jenny, who didn't say a word, just hugged me tight until I couldn't breathe any more. Not the neighbours. Not my boss, Gary, who told me they were coping OK without me and wouldn't expect me back for some time. Not even my mum, whose grief was almost as bad as my own.

I wanted them all to go away and leave me alone.

The only person I wanted to see coming through the door was Harry, and that wasn't ever going to happen again.

The police came, too – two perfectly nice officers offering condolences and explanations I didn't want to hear.

They told me they weren't going to charge the driver with anything, because witnesses had said Harry scooted out into the road without looking, and the car wasn't travelling faster than it should have been. They seemed to think I'd be upset at this, but I knew it wasn't the driver's fault. It was mine, of course, and they couldn't really charge me with anything, could they?

So. Torment. Made worse by two things. Two new things I couldn't get used to.

The first was the trees, which were still screaming, though the more they chopped down the quieter it got. I supposed when the developers reached the last one it would finally stop.

I looked out of the window at them, once, to make sure the noise wasn't just in my head. The site over the road was occupied by a big Edwardian house surrounded by its own grounds – beautiful, it was. I used to imagine it was haunted by the memories of the elegant people who'd lived there. Recently, of course, it had fallen apart, neglected, and the gardens had become overgrown and oppressing.

Despite neighbours' objections, the buyers eventually got permission to knock down the lovely old building and build six new box-like houses in its place. No doubt they'd fetch a lot of money – this was a nice neighbourhood – but everyone with half a heart thought it would be a travesty. The council didn't listen.

Just this week they'd moved in and started to clear the land. I could see them from my bedroom window, chainsaws busy. Cutting.

And the trees were screaming as the saws ripped into their ancient flesh. The only thing that surprised me about this was that no-one else seemed to be able to hear it.

The second thing that kept me wide-eyed all night in those early days were the voices. I could hear them all the time, though they were quieter when no-one was around. Sometimes they were just a faint buzzing, a bit like the chainsaws. But I found it hard to concentrate on anything, because they were always there.

It took me a while, but I finally realised what they were.

When Gerry came to visit – I'd told everyone that I didn't want to see him, but no-one listened to me – I heard him clearly. He was crying, and wringing his hands, and saying how he'd like to help carry the coffin, and I suddenly heard his thoughts, clear as if he was speaking through a megaphone into my ear. *It's your fault... it's your fault... it's your fucking fault.*

Despite his lips saying one thing, the only thought in his head was that it was my fault his only child was dead.

I, too, knew this to be true, but it was still a shock coming from someone else in such a hateful way. No-one else seemed to blame me for what happened. Everyone kept saying it was an accident, as if repeating this over and over meant it would be less of a tragedy.

I recoiled, hurt, but said nothing, even when he insisted he'd have to bring his new girlfriend to the funeral "for moral support." Let him. Nothing mattered any more.

And when Dr Reed returned – apparently he was acting as a locum at the surgery – I heard him, too. He was asking me how I felt – as if I could possibly feel anything at all – and nattering on about time being a healer, and all the usual crap, when his thoughts entered my head, as clear as if he'd just uttered them out loud. *You know, you're really pretty even when you're looking like shit.*

I admit this made me smile a little. Oh, not a proper smile, just a hint of one, but Dr Reed noticed it and stopped prattling on. "You OK?" he asked.

I shook my head. "Of course I'm not," I said. "My baby's dead. It's my fault, and my life will never be worth living ever again."

He fell silent for a moment, a concerned look on his face, then said gently: "The first of those statements is true. The other two are not, although it will take a long time for you to ever realise it."

So that was it, then. I could hear people's thoughts. All the time, whether I wanted to or not. Some were clearer than others, many were confused and erratic, jumping from subject to subject at the blink of an eye, and some people obviously weren't thinking anything at all in a coherent way.

Having so many visitors helped me understand my new-found 'gift' very quickly. I soon found that people had to be quite close for me to 'hear' them properly – if they were in the next room, I could usually hear a mumbling or chattering, but not make out the words.

I also discovered I couldn't turn this ability off. I tried putting my fingers in my ears, but the sounds were just as loud. I tried thinking of something else, to block them out, but I could still hear them.

At night, when I was left alone, there was this faint but irritating buzzing, like a mosquito flying past my ear, and I put this down to hundreds of people's thoughts all around me, as they lay in their beds, sleeping or otherwise. I was listening to people's dreams – and nightmares.

As if I didn't have enough of my own.

Chapter 4

The next day I went to see Harry.

Oh, I didn't want to. How could I want to see my baby unless he was going to smile up at me again? The only thing I wanted, in those early days, was to feel his little hand in mine once more.

No... I didn't want to. But I felt compelled, by my new 'gift' of being able to hear thoughts, to see... well, I know it sounds stupid, and I knew it would be pointless, but I wanted to see if I could hear Harry again. If I could hear his thoughts.

Although I don't believe in an afterlife, or God, or heaven or any of those false hopes mankind has been deceiving himself with for thousands of years, there was just the glimmer of possibility – I didn't dare to call it a hope – that there may still be some of Harry left in that cold, dead body, and that maybe, just maybe, I would be able to hear him one last time before he was destroyed forever.

As I said, I didn't actually have any hope, but once the thought had entered my head I couldn't get rid of it, and I knew I would never rest if I didn't take the opportunity while it still existed.

Everyone tried to put me off, of course. Mum and Andrea had already been to see him, and told me that although he looked perfect he "wasn't Harry any more." Well, I knew that. I'd seen one dead body before, my grandmother, a few years ago, and had noticed then that the resemblance to anyone living was purely coincidental, as they say. The lifeless, white thing lying in her coffin had looked nothing like her, so much so that I nearly told the undertaker he'd shown me to the wrong corpse.

Anyway, I didn't want to actually **see** Harry. I was going to ask them to keep him covered up. I didn't want to add that torment to my already unbearable hell. I just wanted to listen.

So there I was, sitting by his little coffin – so small – and avoiding looking at his little body. His face and body was covered by a white sheet, and I was straining to hear anything – anything – that might be his voice.

I'd asked Jenny, who'd missed another day at work to bring me here, to stay outside in the corridor, and the undertaker was waiting in his office, so I could hear just a muffled, indistinct noise coming from their thoughts, nothing concrete.

There was no-one else around, and the only thing I could hear was my heart beating hard in my chest.

Nothing.

I reached out and, slowly and reluctantly, put a hand on Harry's chest. It felt hard and cold. I wanted to snatch it away, but made myself keep it there. My skin was crawling at the horror of it.

Still nothing.

The silence of the grave.

Sobbing, although I hadn't realised I was doing so, I withdrew my hand and stood up. That was it, then. I would never hear my son's voice ever again, except in my imagination, and the odd video I had of him playing – which wasn't the same thing at all.

Then what, I thought then, was the point of this 'gift' of hearing people's thoughts? So I could hear their pity, their sorrow? Their hatred? What was the point of that?

Harry was dead, and the world was pointless.

…………………………………………..

Harry's funeral was a nightmare of epic proportions. I passed it in a fog of despair, anger and overwhelming guilt. Although it was a complete hell on earth, most of me felt I deserved it, and part of me, paradoxically, never wanted it to end – because when it did, I would have to start 'getting on with my life.'

Because that's what you do, don't you, when someone you love dies? When part of you is taken away, especially suddenly, it's like having an arm or leg brutally ripped from its socket; you are supposed to rage, cry, be sorry, behave in a dignified way throughout the funeral – and then get on with your life.

Well, I didn't feel able to do that.

So, the funeral. Thankfully, apart from the terrible emotions I experienced, I don't remember much about it. It was at a local community hall, where Harry and I had been to several kids' parties in the past. In my memory, the place echoed with happy shouts.

Gerry was there with his girlfriend, but I can't even remember what she looked like. He was crying when I saw him, but I didn't hear his thoughts, thankfully. There were dozens of people there, many of whom I didn't recognise, plenty of whom I've already forgotten, and only one or two things stand out in my memory.

The songs I chose to be played at the beginning and end: The Beatles. It could only be them. Harry loved The Beatles, because I did, of course – we used to sing Yellow Submarine and When I'm 64 in the bath, or at bedtime. But I chose ones he didn't really know, because they had a meaning to me, and he wasn't going to hear them, was he?

I'll Follow The Sun... "One day, you'll look, to see I've gone..." and Golden Slumbers... "Sleep, pretty darling, do not cry..." They had meaning. And as I heard them I knew I'd never be able to play them ever again. I was going to choose Yesterday, but I decided to keep that one for my own personal misery.

So, I remember the music. And the one reading I asked the nice lady conducting Harry's humanist funeral to give, a little note by the famous atheist Richard Dawkins.

Now, I'm not a huge fan of Dawkins; he strikes me as being rather arrogant, and that's one personal trait I dislike. But I've never disagreed with anything he's written, and in his most famous book, The God Delusion, he says: "Being dead will be no different to being unborn – I shall be just as I was in the time of William the Conqueror or the dinosaurs or the trilobites. There is nothing to fear in that."

This is something I've long believed – that we're alive for just a short, unbelievably unlikely, period, whether that's three years like Harry or 103 like some of the luckier ones, and that once we're dead that's it. There is no more, just like there was no before.

I had the humanist lady – I'm sorry, but I can't remember her name – read that out, and talk about Harry, the little character he had managed to become in his short life and, more importantly, how much he meant to the people who loved him. It was pleasant enough, although my insides were being chewed up by despair all through it.

And afterwards we all went home. There was no after-funeral get-together. I didn't want that. Couldn't face that. Everyone had tried to make me organise one, of course – I suppose it's traditional, isn't it? All I got was: "You can't expect people like Uncle John and Aunt

Sarah to come all the way from Oxford for just an hour!" and "You have to let people pay their respects!" Well, they didn't have to come. I wasn't asking them to. They came because they wanted to, for whatever reason.

In the event I think a few of the more distant relatives went to the local pub afterwards. The rest went home, and mum and Andrea came home with me, although I really didn't want them to. I tried to shut out their disapproving thoughts in the taxi on the way back, and when we got home I refused to let them in the house. I went up to my room and shut the door. Shut everyone out.

Alone in my room I could hear nothing. And that's the way I wanted it to stay.

But of course, until that moment when our body dies and we pass from consciousness back into nothingness, our lives are constantly beset with noise, even if it's just our own random thoughts.

With no expectation of peace, I lay on the bed and tried to sleep. At least in sleep we have a few hours' respite.

It was then that the next strange thing happened, making me sit up in wonder.

I forget if I've already mentioned it, but we – sorry, I – have a cat. A sweet little ginger Tom, Jess (Harry named him after Postman Pat's cat – I didn't have the heart to tell him Jess is usually a girl's name; but anyway, I think the cartoon Jess is supposed to be male). We acquired Jess only a few months before Harry's death, after much badgering on his part for a pet, and he loved him wholeheartedly. He'd try to pick him up in that clumsy way kids have, but Jess didn't seem to mind. In fact, he often followed Harry around, and he'd sleep on Harry's bed sometimes. Andrea said this was unhygienic, but I never held to that notion. Cats are generally much cleaner than children.

Anyway, I was lying on the bed, trying to force myself into oblivion, when the door opened and in came Jess. I'd hardly seen him since Harry died – I assumed Andrea had been feeding him, because he'd not been bothering me. He didn't like strange people, and so had probably been hiding away most of the time.

Without thinking, I stretched out my hand so he could nuzzle it in that cute way cats do when they want something – I'm not naïve enough to think it's affection; I don't think cats are capable of that.

They believe in getting what they want, which is fine by me. At least we know where we stand.

So there I was, my hand outstretched, when I heard him, clear as day. *Boy?* he thought.

At least, that was my translation of it. It's hard to put into words, but, like the trees screaming, it was more an emotion than an actual word. The cat was thinking about Harry – wondering where he was, I suppose – and this translated into the word boy.

I sat up, eyes wide, hand frozen in the act of reaching towards this animal that, suddenly, unexpectedly, was communicating with me. I think my jaw dropped open.

Jess came fully into the room, reached my hand and nuzzled it, then thought again: *Boy?*

Instinctively I tickled his ears, like I had done so many times before, and said, tears dripping down my face now: "He's gone away, Jess."

The cat seemed to understand. He jumped up next to me and curled into a ball. I stroked his little fuzzy head, then lay down beside him, my face close to his.

Over the next hour, as I slowly cried myself to sleep, I listened to a cat's simple dreams: of food; of running; of catching a bird; of Harry on his bed.

Chapter 5

The following couple of weeks were, as you can probably imagine if you've ever had a child, the worst in my life. Every night I would go to bed thinking "Harry is dead." Every morning I would wake up after a fitful, nightmare-filled sleep, open my eyes and think "Harry is dead." There was no other reality for me. No solace. No calm. No respite except the couple of hours of nothingness in-between nightmares.

I had some visitors, though I asked for none. Every time someone came I tried to be brave, to hold myself together, for their sake, but every time I ended up sobbing uncontrollably.

There was nothing to live for. No hope for tomorrow, no peace for today.

I even found myself wishing, once or twice, that I had some sort of faith to turn to. I mean, at least those who believe in an afterlife have some hope for the future; some comfort that their loved ones have "gone to a better place," and that they'll see them again some day. I had none.

The only hope I had was of oblivion – that I, too, would one day crumble to dust.

I'd had Harry cremated. I could never bear the thought of his little body decaying in the ground – rather it was reduced to its original state as quickly as possible. I'd left his ashes with the undertaker – at some point in the future I hoped to be strong enough to scatter them in his favourite places, but not yet.

So, I had visitors. Mum came to see me – without Andrea, unusually – the day after the funeral.

Of course I loved my mum – she wasn't a bad woman in any way, and had brought me up well, I think – but she had always been quite cold, and critical of every decision I made. It seems nothing I did was good enough for her. She hated all of my boyfriends (and made sure she told them so), disapproved of me having sex before marriage, and didn't like my career choice (I'm a counsellor: "listening to other people's problems, Steph – is that really a good way to spend your time?" she'd say). Despite the fact she disliked Gerry, and made the fact obvious, she was devastated beyond belief when we got divorced, being of the old school opinion that marriage was for life, even if you hated each other's guts.

She was overjoyed when Harry was born, of course – he was her one and only grandchild, and she doted on him. But she never missed an opportunity to criticise the way I was bringing him up. I was putting him in the cot the wrong way... I should let him cry instead of picking him up... I was feeding him the wrong things... I was letting him watch too much TV... I wasn't teaching him to love God... you get the idea. I tried to ignore it, because Harry adored his Granny, but it was difficult to hold my tongue under the constant barrage.

So when she came to see me – alone for a change – I wasn't exactly expecting a loving and comforting shoulder to cry on.

She brought me some home-made casserole, which I thanked her for, and started by making small talk about this and that; I wasn't really listening, to be honest. After making a cup of tea, we went to sit in the lounge and stared at the walls. Talking to mum had always been difficult – now it seemed impossible.

I was just thinking that the awkward silence couldn't possibly get any more awkward when she spoke, using what I call her school teacher's voice: "Andrea suggested we could have a memorial service for Harry in the church. I thought it was a good idea."

I winced. Not this again. Why couldn't they leave me alone?

"No," I said shortly. My voice was thick with emotion, but she ignored the hint.

"Why ever not? You don't even have to come. It would give us comfort."

I sighed loudly, but said nothing, not trusting myself to answer without anger.

Mum was continuing: "The Reverend says we could have a simple service, with just a few hymns, and prayers, and..."

I couldn't hold it in any longer. Putting my mug of tea down on the coffee table with more force than necessary, I erupted. "Fine!" I shouted. "Do what you like... pray til you're blue in the face, sing songs til your voice cracks... worship your non-existent entity til the church walls fall down... it's not going to bring Harry back, you know! Nothing will!"

Mum was staring at me, horrified. I think I might have actually been frothing at the mouth. I knew I was being unreasonable; that it was my grief talking so angrily, but I couldn't help myself.

She stayed silent, and I suddenly heard her thoughts: *Poor Harry...* and I started sobbing.

She patted me on the arm, and I could tell without looking that she was crying, too.

After a while I calmed down and, through my tears, told her they could have a service if they liked, if it would make them feel better (I genuinely wanted them to find comfort if they could), but I would not be going. Mum seemed pleased, and left soon after.

I went to bed early, and spent the best part of the night staring at the ceiling. Part of me was envious of my mum and sister, and their ability to find comfort in something I never could.

....

Everyone seemed concerned that I should get back to work as soon as possible. Not for the money, you understand – my boss, Gary, had assured me I could take as long as I wanted – but to give me something to focus on. I knew they were right – if I carried on as I was, I would probably go mad pretty soon – but I couldn't face the clients just yet: I had enough problems of my own without having to cope with theirs, too.

I'm a counsellor with a small local organisation. We deal with all types of problems; financial, emotional, but mainly marital. Sometimes we get people referred to us by their GP, social worker or solicitor; otherwise people just find out about us through word of mouth. Some of our clients pay for our services themselves, while others get funded by the relevant authorities.

We talk people through their problems, or, rather, let them talk themselves through – it's better that way; if people can come to their own decisions and resolutions, so much the better.

Most days at work I'd be listening to people rattling on about their husband's dirty habits; their own dirty habits; or their own stupidity. It was hard enough when I was happy and had Harry to cheer me up when I got home. Now he was gone, I'd have nothing but my own misery waiting for me. And there was something more, of course – some new element which I was dreading trying out.

Now, as well as their – usually self-pitying and selfish, often cruel and intolerant – words to listen to, I'd be able to hear their innermost thoughts, too. That was a possibility that filled me with dread.

So I was hoping that this ability I'd awoken with after the trauma of Harry's death would go away as soon as it had arrived. Every morning when I woke up, after the initial "Harry is dead" realisation, I'd listen intently for any evidence of thought-reading, as I had begun to call it.

Living alone, there were usually no distinct sounds at first. And every morning I'd think: "That's it! It's gone!" And then I'd walk downstairs, and the cat would be there at the door, waiting to come in – he usually spent night-time outdoors, chasing rats – and as soon as I opened the door I'd hear him: *Food?*

Cats' thoughts are pretty simple, I find. They only have three needs – food, sleep, and, less often, play. I've always thought it would be nice to be a cat – a well-fed, well looked-after one, naturally – and I found it really easy to hear what he was thinking. To be honest, he didn't think much at all. No theologising for him. No worrying about where his next meal was coming from. No wondering about the point of his existence. No fretting about the future. Lucky bastard.

I supposed most animals would be the same, except maybe the most intelligent ones such as apes, dolphins and elephants. Driven by instinct, their thoughts would focus on the present, and what they needed to stay happy. How I wished, then, that we could be like that.

Instead, I had to listen to the random, often pointless, thoughts of everyone who crossed my path. Mum, telling me for the fifteenth time that I had to think of other people as well as myself, her mind thinking: *Just get a grip, Stephanie, and we can all go back to normal.*

Andrea, trying to get me, once again, to see her beloved Reverend Cooper, thinking: *Come on, come on – use this to find God, please!*

The nice Gary from work, who came to reassure me he would hold my position for as long as it took, bizarrely thinking about how he was going to shag his wife later that day. I think he saw me blushing, but of course didn't know why. As he was leaving, I told him to "remember me to Sue," and couldn't help smiling.

Then there was the window cleaner, who always gave me the creeps and struck me as a bit of a perve, shocking me by thinking nothing but kind thoughts when he came to collect his money, even though I only had a dressing gown on at the time. It made me realise that you really couldn't judge a book by its cover – this was something I'd always professed to know, but in reality I was just as judgemental as the next man. Not any more.

These were the only people I met in the first week after the funeral. I didn't leave the house, spending most of my time listening blankly to the radio or staring out of the window.

Mum and Andrea got my shopping, made most of my food – though I ate very little – and dealt with my bills, etc. I know it was kind of them, but in a way it just made me worse – instead of having to do things for myself, they took over. Mind you, I really believe I would have starved to death if someone hadn't been forcing food onto my plate. I cared that little about the future.

The second week was a little better. I suppose the numbness and shock starts to wear off, however traumatic the experience, and the body begins to revert to survival mode. I began to eat a little more. I picked up a book and read a couple of paragraphs. I even contemplated leaving the house.

On the Wednesday of that week I woke up, leapt out of bed for the first time in ages, got dressed, let the cat in, fed him – according to his demands – and, without eating or drinking anything, took my courage into my own hands and went outside.

I can't say I'd had a sudden revelation, or anything like that, but I had come to realise that if I carried on the way I was I would just waste away – and that Harry, if he had been around to see me, would have been appalled. Harry had loved me unconditionally, as children do, and he had hated it when I was sick, or sad, or lonely. He'd come and sit on my knee, and cuddle me, and stroke my hair, and whisper "Don't cry, mummy." How I needed him here, now.

He wasn't here, but somehow I still felt the need to be a better person because of him.

Does that make sense? Probably not, but it felt like my salvation.

It was a nice morning, sunny if a bit cold, and the light hurt my eyes as I walked down the road towards the woods. Back in the old days, before Harry was born and I had more time to myself, I used to do a lot of walking. It always cleared my head, helped me think through any problems I had, as well as making my body feel better.

Maybe this time would be no different.

Feeling a little strange, I strode through the tree-lined streets, past the post office on the corner, meeting no-one. Occasionally people's thoughts buzzed through my head like bees, but they were always too far away to be distinct. I'd catch the odd word, then they were gone.

When I reached the woods I turned along the path towards the kennels, and stopped. With my ears I could hear plenty of things – birdsong, distant cars along the main road to the right, and, louder now, the incessant barking of the dozen or so dogs caged up in the kennels.

This constant barking used to distress me even back in the days when I could only hear sounds. I'd think about the poor imprisoned dogs, believing themselves no doubt to be abandoned by their owners, all vying for attention, or food, or just to be heard above the others. It always struck me as a particularly cruel place to put your pet, even for a couple of days.

Now, as I slowly drew nearer to the grey rectangular building that jutted out into the woodland path, my fears were magnified tenfold. Now I couldn't just hear their barking, I could hear their simple thoughts as well.

Food! Food! Food! went several. *Man! Man!* went another, higher pitched, one. *Walk! Walk! Walk!* and, more heart-breakingly, just *Out* repeated over and over and over…

I covered my ears, pointlessly, and walked as quickly as I could down the path, past the kennels. Anything to get away from this misery. How could we be so cruel to animals we were supposed to love?

As the barking and the thoughts faded, I started to think about the implications of this new ability of mine. Presuming no-one else in the world could hear the things I could – and I had no reason to believe anyone could – did I not have a responsibility to tell people? To let them know what our animals were thinking? More importantly, to let them know how our animals were suffering?

With horror, I realised that if I ever visited a farm or – worse still – a slaughterhouse, I would be plunged into unimaginable terror.

I resolved, then, to do something about it. I was either going to lose this ability, somehow, or, if I was cursed with it forever, I would use it to bring some form of good to the world. How, I had no idea, but at least it would be something to aim for.

Something to live for.

Chapter 6

Over the next few days I spent hours just walking. I had a route I took, through the residential area, into the woods – quickly past the kennels, with their sad and incessant calls for help – and on into the park.

Our local park is a large one, with its own lake in the middle, and a circular path that I reckon is around a mile-and-a-half long. I'd get on this path and just walk, one foot in front of the other, mechanically travelling in mind as well as place.

I noticed little about my surroundings. The trees were quiet – no chainsaws here – apart from the birds' calls, and it's far enough away from any traffic noise. I met a few people, of course, but these were mainly dog-walkers or pensioners out for a stroll, and their thoughts were quiet ones. Sometimes I'd hear someone singing in their head, and it would make me smile a little. Others would be thinking about what they were going to have for lunch, or about how nice the weather was – it was all, thankfully, pretty mundane stuff.

On one occasion I passed an old lady shuffling along with her tiny dog, and I heard her thinking about her husband, *dear Albert*, who had died some time ago. She was remembering how he used to dance with her, even though he hated dancing... *two left feet, silly old sod...* It made me sad, and I wished for the umpteenth time that week that I could be left alone with my own thoughts. They were sad enough.

On one of these walks I sat by the lake for a while, the sun on my back, and watched the ducks and geese squabbling over some bread a little girl had thrown. As they grew nearer, the bread tossed and ripped between their beaks, I could hear their thoughts. *Food! Mine! Food! Mine!* Lives so simple. If only.

The glare on the water made my eyes ache, so I got up and moved on, leaving the birds to their quarrel.

All this walking gave me space to think, about what I was going to achieve now I was on my own again, about what I wanted to do with this extraordinary ability I had suddenly acquired.

Over the course of a few days, I decided I would first of all try to get rid of it.

As far as I could see, it could serve no useful purpose – wouldn't save any lives, or even make them better. Maybe if I was an international diplomat (a career I seemed unlikely to achieve at this late stage in life) I could use the ability to help bring about world peace. I assumed it would be rather useful to know what other people were thinking in some circumstances.

But I was just a normal person, with a normal job and normal connections. It was unlikely my being able to hear Joe from the Post Office's desire for a cheese sandwich *and maybe a Mars bar... the diet can start on Monday...* would prove earth-shattering in any way.

So I decided I wanted, if possible, to get rid of it. To be free.

But how?

That night I logged on to my computer for the first time since Harry died and Googled "hearing voices" and "thought-reading," then "telepathy" for good measure, plus a myriad of combinations of these ideas. I came up with nothing positive except several suggestions I may be going mad (quite possible, of course), was psychotic, or had a brain tumour (equally possible, though I hadn't had any other symptoms). I could find no evidence that anyone else (at least, anyone sane) in the known universe actually believed telepathy was possible.

So maybe I **was** going mad. Or had a tumour. How could I find out?

The next day I made an appointment to see Dr Reed, the nice-looking doctor who had been so kind as to knock me out with pills after Harry's death. I had no intention of telling him I could hear thoughts – apart from anything else, I didn't want to end up being poked and prodded any more than was necessary, thank you very much, and I certainly didn't want to be forcefully evicted to a place where the furniture is nicely padded – but I decided to say I'd been getting bad headaches. This little white lie would hopefully prompt a brain scan, which would, I hoped, pick up any abnormalities.

If my ability was brought about by something physical, maybe they could fix it. Remove it. I didn't really have a clue, and I knew I was clutching at straws, but at least I felt I was doing something.

I told the doctor's receptionist I was in pain and needed to see a doctor as soon as possible, so naturally she said they didn't have an appointment for four days. I told her as long as it was with Dr Reed, that was fine.

Four days later I was sitting in the waiting room, listening to the miserable thoughts of those around me. Jeeze, how self-pitying some people can be! Mr Turnbull, who used to work in the local shop before he retired, was there with his wife, and all I could hear coming from his head was an endless list of ailments – bad legs, bad knees, bad back, bad eyes, bad ears... I'm surprised he hadn't fallen apart. His wife, by contrast, was only thinking of him, and how she was going to make him a nice supper with his favourite pudding to cheer him up. She'd be lucky.

Next to me was a young girl with a new baby, whose thoughts were particularly upsetting. She was obviously sleep-deprived, with dark circles around her eyes and hair unbrushed. Her baby was grizzling on her lap, wrapped in a blue blanket, but she wasn't paying it much attention, her eyes gazing instead out of the window, though there was precious little to see there, just a car park and a couple of trees.

Her thoughts were slow and tired, just like her: *I can't do this... anymore... I can't take it anymore... I can't... what about Mark? Mark would make it all better... so tired... so... I could just leave him here, couldn't I? They'd look after him better than me. So...*

I turned to look at her properly. Her hands were twitching the baby's blanket, picking at it nervously, and she looked terrible. She looks worse than me, I thought... and suddenly wondered if she could hear **my** thoughts. It made me laugh a little, and the girl looked at me suspiciously.

"Sorry," I mumbled. "Just remembered a joke."

She said nothing, but I could hear her loud and clear: *Can't remember when I laughed last... so tired... so...*

I was going to say something more to her – I don't know what, really – but just then the electronic voice boomed out from the speakers: "Stephanie Martin to Dr Reed in Room 4... Stephanie Martin to Dr Reed in Room 4."

I went, knocking gently on the half-open door before going in.

Dr Reed was sitting at his desk, looking at a computer screen, and as I entered he looked up, turned towards me and gestured for me to sit down.

"And what can I do for you today, Ms Martin?" he asked. His voice was gentle, his eyes as kind as I remembered them.

I sat down, and for a moment couldn't for the life of me remember why I had come. Then it came to me.

"Headaches!" I stuttered, rather too loudly.

He looked a tad alarmed. "Sorry?" he said.

I nearly laughed again, but managed to contain it into a half smile. "I'm sorry," I said. "I've been having headaches, really bad ones, and they won't go away, even with painkillers." I'd read that if you have continuous headaches that don't improve with normal painkillers it could be a sign of something bad, and wanted to milk this a bit.

Dr Reed picked up his blood pressure monitor and stood up. "How long has this been going on?" he said, waiting for me to remove my coat before securing the cuff around my upper arm.

"Oh, about a week," I lied, as he inflated it. "And where are the headaches situated?" I had to think about this one. "Erm... in the front of my head," I said, making it up on the spot.

As he took my blood pressure I tried to listen to his thoughts, but all I got was an indistinct jumble. Presumably he was thinking of possible diagnoses.

He removed the cuff. "Blood pressure's normal," he said, then turned to look at my notes on the screen. "Have you been taking those anti-depressants I prescribed you?"

I bridled a bit. "No, thank you," I said. "I don't want to take pills." Not unless they're going to take away reality, I thought... and smiled inwardly, thinking maybe they would do just that, if only I had the guts to take them.

Dr Reed looked serious. "It's just headaches could have been a side-effect of the pills," he said, and got up again to shine a light in my eyes. "Where exactly is the pain?"

I indicated a point just to the right of my temple. He put his hands gently on my head and rubbed a little. "Does it hurt when I do this?" he asked.

I looked up at him and for a minute couldn't think what to say. "Er.. no, it just hurts all the time," I lied. He nodded, took his hands away and sat down.

"It's probably just the stress you're experiencing," he said, beginning to type something on his keyboard. "I'll prescribe you some strong painkillers, and if they don't work then come back in three days."

Oh great. No brain scan, then. At least not yet. It seemed I would have to keep this pretence up for some time if I wanted the NHS to look into my new-found gift.

I thought of telling him then, I really did – I mean, he was so nice, and seemed so understanding – but I knew he'd just think I was crazy, and I didn't want him to think that. So what I did next was a bit strange, to be honest.

I took the prescription he printed out, thanked him, promised I'd be back in three days if the pills didn't work (of course they wouldn't!) and then, as I put my coat back on and got up to leave, said: "There's a girl in the waiting room with a new baby. Is she coming to see you?"

The doctor looked a bit confused, turned to his computer again, checked something then said: "Yes, she is, why?" I turned back to face him, my hand on the door handle.

"Because I think she's got post-natal depression. She's certainly sleep-deprived. And she's thinking about abandoning her baby here."

Chapter 7

I have to say I kept kicking myself about that in the days following my visit to the doctor's. His face! I told myself he must have assumed I'd been speaking to the girl with the baby, not listening to her thoughts. But that was little consolation. I'd as much as told him!

Of course I didn't take the pills, and the imaginary headaches continued (in fact they got worse, would you believe it?), so I made an appointment after three days to see Dr Reed again. This time I was going to lay it on thick, saying I'd had blurred vision, and adding that I'd been vomiting as well (I hadn't), as this would, I believe, lead him to book me in for a scan.

After I'd told him how bad it was, he looked serious again, examined me (fruitlessly, of course), asked me a load of questions and said he'd send me for a CT scan to see if anything would show up, while reassuring me it was probably just migraines. I even felt sorry for him, he looked so worried.

Anyhow, the scan was booked for the following week, and I duly went along, lay down in the required place and let a machine look into my brain. As I was lying there, I could hear the jumbled thoughts of the hundreds of people in the hospital, and it made me even more determined to get rid of this 'gift.' I couldn't take much more of this.

A week later I was back in Dr Reed's surgery. I assumed they hadn't found anything drastic – after all, no-one had called me in straight away, I'd had to chase the results – but felt I had to go and keep up the pretence.

The good doctor smiled at me as I went in, and I took from that I wasn't dying of a tumour or something.

"It's good news," he said, as I sat down. "There was nothing on your scan to indicate any abnormality." Oh great, I thought, I'm normal? Part of me was relieved, naturally, while the greater part of me was disappointed there was nothing physical to correspond with my thought-reading abilities.

The disappointment must have shown in my face, for Dr Reed looked confused. "I said you're normal," he reiterated. "The scan results were negative for any indication of a bleed or tumour."

I tried to smile. "Great," I said, weakly.

Dr Reed stopped in his tracks, and surprised me by taking my hand, which was resting on the desk. "What's wrong, Stephanie?" he asked, gently.

I looked up at him, so handsome and caring, and just dissolved into tears like a simpering idiot. I snatched my hand away from his (surely there was some law about not touching your patients, I idly thought) and put it to my face, covering my eyes, trying to hide my misery.

Dr Reed just let me cry, which I did for maybe five minutes before regaining composure and wiping my tears on a tissue he offered me. I looked at him, and, for the first time, could hear him thinking: *Poor girl. Poor, poor girl.*

This made me cry even more. For some reason, whenever I've been upset in the past it has always been other people's sympathy which has caused me to erupt into self-pity.

In-between my tears I realised he was speaking, too. "It's OK," he said. "It's most probably just tension headaches, caused by your recent loss, and the stress involved. I think you might benefit from counselling. I can recommend someone if you like."

I guffawed, then – actually snorted with laughter – at the irony. Me, a counsellor, needing my own services! Of course I wouldn't benefit from counselling. I knew exactly what I'd tell myself, and it was all to no avail. The only thing that would help me now was silencing the voices in my head, and it looked like that would never happen. At least, not until I joined Harry in Oblivion.

I almost told him then. I almost opened up to Dr Reed (I still didn't know his first name) and let him in on my secret, but I didn't. I was afraid of what he'd say, what he'd do... how he'd look at me. Aside from all other considerations, that was what bothered me most – how he'd look at me.

So I said nothing.

....

The following week I went back to work.

At first it was torture, because everyone either avoided me in embarrassment at not knowing what to say, or else kept treating me like a child, telling me I looked well and saying things like "Time is a great healer" and other platitudes.

It reminded me of the time, years ago, when I went into work after smacking my face on a cupboard door (yes, it does happen) and gaining a rather fetching black eye. I was still with Gerry at the time, and everyone must have assumed he'd been knocking me around, because no-one – and I mean no-one – even mentioned my black and blue face.

I mean, it was literally purple. People's eyes just seemed to pass over it, as if it was nothing, and not a single colleague (a couple of whom I regarded as friends) said a dicky bird. That taught me a great deal about people, I tell you. Only one person – a client who had a history of violence – commented on my disfigurement. He asked me if my "old man" had been laying down the law lately. I told him the truth, and he seemed disappointed.

So I went back to work. I mean, there was little else to do with my life now Harry was... now I no longer had Harry to look after. And I still had bills to pay, even if there was just me now.

My first client when I got back was an elderly lady with anxiety issues, who I'd seen many times before. Mrs Barrett was 75, hunched and huddled, with grey curly hair and a walking stick. The proverbial little old lady, she seemed to try to live up to her stereotype by wearing shapeless patterned dresses, carrying a battered old handbag and saying "sorry dear?" a lot. I think Gary made sure I saw her because she was always easy to deal with; to be honest I think she only came for the company, we were never much help.

In fact I kept telling her not to waste her money on any more appointments. "Mrs Barrett," I'd say, "I really do feel there's no further progress we can make regarding your issues. You just need to continue making an effort to get out more. How's that flower arranging class coming on?" And so on.

But she'd just look at me over the top of her glasses (naturally), shake her head gently, disturbing a snow flurry of dandruff, and say "But I feel we're getting somewhere. Have I ever told you about my troubled childhood?" Then she'd launch into an account of her upbringing, the death of her mother when she was 15 and her father's gambling habit. I know I sound unsympathetic, but I'm really not – she had got over these issues a long time ago, and her problems now stemmed from the fact her family lived elsewhere, seldom came to see her, and her friends were all dying. It's called getting old in today's society.

So I was a bit relieved when she arrived, as usual on time, and flung her handbag to the floor. "Well," she said, "I haven't seen you for a while. You been ill?" Then, before waiting for an answer (thankfully) she started moaning about being on her own, berating her son for never coming to see her and crying a little over another friend who had "gone to meet her maker," as she put it.

I hardly got a word in edgeways, and was amused to hear her thoughts, in her quieter moments, seemed to revolve around what she was going to have for tea (a microwave cottage pie, followed by one of those nice cakes she'd got from Tesco's) and the edition of Jeremy Kyle she'd seen that morning (*that woman!*) It was honestly like her tongue wasn't connected to her brain. I don't suppose many people's are…

Our session lasted an hour, at the end of which I felt decidedly more positive. I'd got through my first client without my new-found ability being too much trouble; maybe they'd all be like that. Unfortunately, that wasn't to be.

My next clients were a married couple – let's call them Stuart and Susan McDonough, for those were their names. I'd never seen them before, as they had only started coming to us a couple of weeks ago. Reading their case notes beforehand, I saw they'd been referred by their solicitor after starting divorce proceedings, as the solicitor thought they had 'unresolved issues' which needed to be sorted out before they split.

Their problems included the husband's adultery with several women, the wife's inability to accept the relationship was over, and the couple's disagreement over who would get custody of their two young children. It was a typical situation I'd seen plenty of times before, which of course was never easy to resolve. The best you could hope for was for them to agree to disagree, but when children were involved it always complicated matters.

As soon as they walked in I could hear their thoughts. Susan, a small, mousy sort of woman in her early 30s, wearing badly fitting, rather shabby clothes and with messy, greying hair tied up in an untidy and unfashionable ponytail, was clearly terrified. As she sat down, acknowledging my welcome and putting a plastic bag full of god knows what on the floor next to her chair, I could hear her repeating the same thing over and over: *This is not a good idea. This is not a good idea.*

Her husband, on the other hand, just seemed furious. He had obviously been forced to attend, which is never a good start, and he didn't even say hello as he sat down heavily on the chair offered to him. Even without the telepathy I would have been able to read him like a book – after all, it's part of my training. Dressed in dirty jeans and a t-shirt which read "Life's a piece of shit" (nice one, I thought, though wondering if it was a reference to Monty Python), he stared at me with undisguised hatred and started mumbling under his breath. Why the hell did Gary give me **this** case? I asked myself, but it was no use wondering – it's the luck of the draw whether you get a decent client or not.

But it was his thoughts which worried me, and caused me to mentally check where the panic button we all have under our desks was situated, making sure it was within reach when I sat down.

It was just one word, repeated over and over like a stuck record. For some reason it made me remember the trees, screaming – something I had tried very hard to dismiss from my memory.

Bitch. Bitch. Bitch. Bitch. Bitch.

Chapter 8

That first session with the McDonoughs was disturbing yet uneventful. If only I had known then what would happen later, I would have played it differently; but well, hindsight's a great thing.

I continued to work, a bit mechanically, I have to say – going through the motions, if you like, saying what had to be said and not really concentrating much. I don't suppose it could have been any other way, really. As a counsellor myself, who'd read all the relevant textbooks (some of them more than once!) I knew grief wasn't something you could just put away on a shelf, like an old toy. It was with you constantly for quite some time – years in some cases, forever in others – like an unwelcome virus which sapped your energy and crept up on you when you least expected it.

I'd be talking to a client about something totally unrelated – their diminishing sex life, for example – and suddenly find myself thinking about something Harry had said, or remember his face looking up at me, all smiles, or the way he shouted at his toys when he was annoyed I wouldn't let him have another biscuit. It was most bizarre, and I often had to struggle to get my thoughts back on track.

In a way I was glad to have the added distraction of other people's thoughts bombarding me, because although undoubtedly related to Harry's death it seemed totally unconnected – it was nothing to do with Harry, nothing to do with the way he died, just a freak consequence. Something my brain had decided to do after the shock it had endured.

I couldn't rationalise it – as you can probably guess, I had never held with superstition or beliefs in the spiritual or paranormal; as far as I was concerned it was all nonsense. I used to make a point of walking under ladders, putting an umbrella up indoors and leaving my shoes on the table, precisely because my mother told me doing such things was unlucky. Really…

So this was a bit of a turn-up for the books, as they say. I couldn't explain it, couldn't understand why or how it had happened – it just was, and I supposed I'd have to get used to it if it didn't go away.

Over the coming months I stopped thinking of it as a burden, and started to regard it as a tool. Not quite a bonus, not yet, but as something I could learn to use to my advantage. I could certainly use it in my job, by listening to what people were really thinking when their mouths were saying something else. As you can imagine, that ability could come in really handy for someone trying to get inside another person's mind.

To give you an example, one of my regular clients was a 20-something lad who had anger issues, addictions to both alcohol and gambling, and the apparent inability to form any sort of meaningful relationships. He was sent to us by his parents, a successful middle-class couple who were distraught at the way their only child had turned out.

Jacob had underachieved at school, shown no interest in getting any sort of job, had never had a girlfriend and had by degrees retreated into his room, where he slept a lot. In his waking hours – usually when his parents were asleep – he gambled online and drank large quantities of cheap but potent alcohol. The money he required to fund his bad habits came, naturally, from his well-meaning but pretty hopeless parents, who had given him everything he needed from an early age and weren't prepared to give up now.

At our previous sessions he had been, not surprisingly, uncommunicative, speaking in monosyllables and grunting a lot. It had been like getting blood out of the proverbial stone, and I was all for telling his parents that they were wasting their money.

However, our first session after my return to work was, shall we say, a little different.

"Jacob," I said, cheerfully, as he entered the room. "How are you today?"

The lad shuffled in as usual, plonked himself down in the chair I indicated to him and crossed his arms sulkily. Nothing unusual here, then. I knew he only agreed to come to these sessions because his dad had threatened to withdraw his internet access if he refused.

"So, Jacob," I resumed. "What would you like to talk about today?" We often used this approach with clients, asking them to bring up what was most on their minds. Sometimes it worked, other times not, but it was my best bet with someone like Jacob.

The youth looked over at me with his brown eyes. He really was quite attractive, though he obviously didn't think so, with long wavy brown hair, although the years indoors had made his skin sallow and dry.

I smiled at him. He mumbled something I didn't catch, but I heard his thought as clear as day: *Elaine.*

"Sorry?" I asked.

"I said I don't want to talk about anything," he replied. This was what he usually said, though this time I knew otherwise.

"OK," I resumed. "How about **I** talk and you join in when you want to." He nodded at this, but rolled his eyes.

"Well, I hear your mum's got a new job," I went on. He shrugged his shoulders. "At the local vets, yes?"

"Yes."

"Does that mean she's earning more money?"

"No."

"Oh?"

"Less," he said. Still the monotone.

"Does it mean she's at home more?"

"I dunno."

"I expect she wants to spend more time with you?"

"I dunno."

This was getting me nowhere. How could I find out who Elaine was without downright asking him? I couldn't even ask his mum or dad – client confidentiality, plus of course the not wanting to have to explain where I got the name from, put paid to that. I'd just have to keep fishing for clues.

"Have you made any new friends lately?"

"No."

"Not online?" I knew many of his 'friends' were virtual ones.

"No."

"Been out at all?"

"The shop." Aha.

"The newsagent's?"

"No-one calls it that. The shop. For food," *crisps and cider. And Elaine.*

Those last words, unspoken but heard nonetheless, said so much.

I took a gamble myself, then. "I hear there's a new girl working at the shop." I had no way of knowing this – I wasn't even sure which shop he meant, though we lived pretty close – but felt it was worth a try. After all, those corner shops were always getting new staff in.

He blushed a little. Actually blushed! And I knew I'd struck lucky.

"Maybe."

"You like her?"

"Shut up," he said, but not in a rude way, more an awkward kid way.

"Maybe you should ask her out?"

"I don't think so, Miss," he said. He always called me Miss, like I was his teacher. I took it, of course, as a sign of his immaturity, and let him. As long as clients are polite they can call me what they want.

"Why not?" I asked. "Does she have a boyfriend?"

He blushed again, shrugged his shoulders. "I dunno."

"Well you'll never find out if you don't ask."

The thoughts again: *Too scared.*

"What are you scared of?"

He looked at me with those beautiful yet lost brown eyes again. "Rejection," he said.

I smiled. "Rejection won't kill you. She can only say no. And if she does, at least you'll know how she feels. And if she doesn't..."

He stayed silent, and I carried on: "You may find out she likes you, too. Stranger things have happened."

"I suppose." My, this was progress.

We spent the rest of the session talking about different things – well, **I** talked about different things, mainly – but I sensed he felt a little more positive, and when he was leaving I said: "Think about asking that girl out, Jacob. Sometimes we have to be brave in order to make ourselves happy. What have you got to lose?"

He shrugged, which I took as a reply, and left the room.

I sat down at my desk to write up the notes on the session, and after a while thinking wrote: "Some progress made."

Chapter 9

That weekend, the first after my return to work, Andrea came round to see me. Oh, I didn't ask her to – didn't want her to, to be honest. She always drove me mad, brought out the worst in me, and now I could hear her unspoken thoughts as well as her spoken ones, I could hardly bear to be in the same room as her.

However, she was my sister, so I couldn't really object.

She rang me up on the Thursday evening, and asked if she could come around on Saturday afternoon. I tried to say I was busy, but she knew I wasn't, so I had to agree.

Funnily enough, it was while she was on the phone that I realised I couldn't hear any thoughts from her. Even in our silences – and there were a few of those, I can tell you – there was nothing. No disapproving *Get a grip, girl* or patronising *God take pity on her* – just silence.

So maybe I couldn't hear thoughts over the phone lines, or satellite waves, or however the hell phones work these days. Perhaps I had to be in the same place as someone to 'hear' them. Well, that was certainly something to be thankful for, I concluded. Maybe I could confine any future relationships to the phone. Although it may make sex difficult. I snorted laughing.

"What's that?" asked Andrea. She didn't like laughter. It disturbed her sense of the seriousness of life.

"Nothing," I lied. "The cat's just fallen off the sofa."

"Hmph," she said. Andrea didn't like animals – thought they were dirty, smelly and a waste of time and money, particularly money.

"So," I resumed, "What time are you coming round then?"

"About three. I won't stay for tea." Oh good.

"Oh that's a shame," I said. "Is Tim coming with you?" Tim is Andrea's husband, a Bible-bashing, God-fearing, bigoted, racist and thoroughly unpleasant man who I detested on sight. He was one of those people who did whatever he liked, but believed everyone else would go to Hell if they did the same. Hypocrite didn't come close.

"Oh no," Thank you, baby Jesus. "he's got a class to go to." I didn't ask, and I didn't want to know, what sort of a class. Jewthumping or Muslim-assaulting, presumably. I nearly laughed again, and ended the call in a hurry. Even my stupid cat wouldn't fall off the sofa twice.

On Saturday Andrea was bang on time, as usual. One thing you can say about my sister, she's very punctual. I think she believes it's a Godly thing to be, though why I've no idea. I can't remember one of the Ten Commandments being Thou Shalt Never Leave Anyone Waiting.

Whatever, she arrived on time, with a bunch of daffodils in one hand and a fussy grey handbag in the other. Once I'd let her in she barged her way into the kitchen, grabbed a vase and started to unwrap the flowers.

"Are they for me?" I asked. Maybe she was going to take them home again.

Andrea looked sideways at me, and I heard her think: *God you're looking old.* Well, thanks, Sis, I actually thought I was pretty OK-looking today. "Of course they're for you," she snapped, putting them carelessly in the vase and adding water from the tap, before sitting down at the kitchen table.

"I'll put the kettle on, shall I?" I asked, getting two mugs out of the cupboard.

"Please. Tea, three sugars."

"Yes, I know."

As I was making the tea – Andrea had always liked it unfeasibly sweet, ever since she was a child – she removed her coat and scarf, flung them on the back of the chair, then started telling me what she and Tim had been up to recently. This seemed to involve terrorising local children, brainwashing them into believing they were destined for eternal damnation if they so much as told a lie, as well as patronising the children's parents and sucking up to the vicar.

The pair were heavily involved in running a weekly children's club at their church – I took Harry once, only because I had no other babysitter at the time, and I was desperate, and he came home talking about sin. He was two-and-a-half years old. I nearly slapped Andrea in the ensuing row.

"So, how are you getting on at work?" she asked, once she'd given me the rundown of what was happening in church.

"Oh, you know, it's like I've never been away," I said, though this was not strictly true.

"I hope they're not giving you difficult cases to deal with."

"Well, people don't come to us with a splinter in their thumb, Andrea," I replied. "They wouldn't need a counsellor if their cases weren't difficult."

She tutted. "I mean I hope they're not giving you bereaved people to deal with," she said. "You're not fit to deal with people who've been bereaved, are you?"

I started. "Excuse me?"

"I mean," she simpered, in that wheedling little voice which always made me want to strangle her with her own scarf, "you've got enough of your own grief to deal with at the moment without taking on other people's too." While this was undoubtedly true, it somehow angered me.

"I would have thought that the best person to talk about grief is someone who has been through it themselves," I countered.

"Ah yes," she said, "but you can't talk to anyone about what really happens to our departed, can you? About how to pray for their souls, or offer them hope about seeing their loved ones in the next life?"

Oh here we go again, I thought.

"No, Andrea, I can't. Because I can't bullshit people about an imaginary afterlife like you could."

Great, we hadn't even drunk our tea yet and we were starting a row. I didn't have to look into her reddening face to see she was getting angrier by the second – and I could hear her thinking *Dear God, why is she so unbelieving? Why did you make her thus, if you made everything?*

I smiled a little at that, which only served to annoy her more.

"How can you not believe, Steph? How can you look at this wonderful world of ours and not see that it has to have been created by someone better than us?"

Very easily, I thought, but I said: "We've been through this before, many times." I was suddenly very tired.

"I know," she said. "And it grieves me. It grieves God to see you so adamant that your version of the truth is the right one."

"Well, let him come visit me and maybe I'll believe in him," I said.

"God does not need to prove he exists, he just does."

"Well isn't that convenient. Sometimes I think there is a God, and he just doesn't like us."

"Whether you believe in him or not, he still loves you." *He loves us all.*

"Is that so?" I asked.

"Of course. God loves all of his creation." *Even you, Steph.*

"Really?"

"Yes." *God show her the way.*

I had her here. "Does God love that man in America, the one who went into that school and shot dead 15 little children and three of their teachers last week?"

"Well..." *Of course not*, she thought.

"And how about that guy in the paper a couple of weeks ago who tortured four women before raping them and slitting their throats? Did God make him, too?"

Stop it, she was thinking. But I couldn't.

"And how about that poor Syrian man whose wife, mother, sister and five children drowned in front of him when their boat overturned on their way to Greece? Does God love him? Did God love his children?" I had started silently crying by then, tears trickling down my nose and falling into my untouched tea. "Or the people who live every day with unbearable physical pain – does he love them?"

"Well, God moves in mysterious ways," she flustered.

"Too fucking right he does."

"Please don't swear, Steph." She had two hands wrapped round her mug, but had yet to take a sip.

"Your 'god' makes me swear," I said. "The thought that anyone can still believe in an all-powerful, loving god when there's so much unnecessary suffering in the world makes me laugh. Or cry, or something."

She was praying in her head again, and it just infuriated me more. I continued my rant: "If your God really does see everything, and direct everything, why does he let so much shit go on? Why does he make innocent, well-meaning people suffer unbearable things on a daily basis?"

She couldn't answer. Not even someone of her unfailing belief knew the answer to that one. Then I hit her with the killer:

"Did God love Harry, Andrea?"

She stopped mid-prayer, and turned her face to look at me. "Of course he did. God loves everyone."

"Well, he has a funny fucking way of showing it."

....……..

Thankfully, our conversation moved on to more mundane matters after that. Andrea moaned about mum, about the price of food ("proper fresh veg is so hard to get these days. I mean, you can't trust that stuff from the supermarket, can you?") and about Tim's job – he's a head teacher, would you believe. I can't think of a less suitable person I'd like to teach any child of mine, except Donald Trump, maybe, or Hitler.

Andrea herself doesn't work, believing a Christian woman's place is in the home, looking after the house and children, though they've never had any kids – not through choice, I believe – and she has a cleaner to do most of the housework. What she does all day I don't know. Knit Bibles for African heathens, probably.

Anyway, I managed to get rid of her an hour-and-a-half after she arrived. I was sure she wanted to go, anyway: She'd given up on saving my soul for the day.

As she was heading out of the door her mouth was telling me to look after myself, while her brain was still thinking about her God and his love. Sometimes I envied her.

God loves you, Steph.

Yeah, right.

Chapter 10

The following week Jenny came to visit me. We'd been friends since secondary school, and usually saw each other every month or so, going to the cinema or theatre, maybe bowling, sometimes just the pub. She had come to see me several times just after Harry died, but we'd since fallen back into the old routine.

It was amazing to me how quickly things returned to normal after Harry's death. In many ways it was like nothing had changed, when to me everything had. I suppose to the rest of the world, even those who knew him, existence was the same. So little does one life truly matter to anyone but itself and those closest to it.

I had often thought you could look at it this way: If every life on earth was a burning candle, you'd never notice the ones that were extinguished, especially as more were being added every second. Life goes on, as the saying goes.

Except I, being so close to the candle that was so quickly and cruelly blown out, was left in the dark.

Jenny tried to bring a little light back. She had always been a caring friend – I had many 'friends' who I barely saw from one year to the next, and who I swear would never contact me again if I left them to it. I choose to believe that says more about them than it does about me. I hope I'm right.

Jenny is different. She rings me regularly, always asking what she can do for me, not the other way around. She just seems to know when I need her support, and never fails to make me laugh. The best type of best friend.

She arrived on the Wednesday evening, about 7, with a big bar of my favourite chocolate and a bottle of wine. I didn't really want either, just yet, but it was a nice thought.

"How's work?" she asked, once we had settled down in the lounge. Everyone asked me that at the time – as if work was at least a safe subject to raise.

"It's OK," I said. "Pretty uneventful." This wasn't true, as you can imagine, but obviously I couldn't tell her about the extra element it now involved.

"Any interesting new cases?" Jenny was always genuinely interested in my work, having had a passing desire to go into that line of business herself in our teenage years. As it was she had eventually settled on nursing instead, and now worked in our local hospital.

"Not really," I replied. "Although even if I did, you know I couldn't tell you about them."

She laughed. "Of course. If you told me about them you'd have to kill me afterwards." She flushed, then, and I heard her thoughts: *Oh sorry, Steph.* "I'm sorry," she said, quietly.

"It's OK, Jen..." I was going to go on, but couldn't. I got up instead. "Fancy some of that wine?" I asked.

"Er... just a tea, please," she said. I was a bit taken aback. Jenny always drank alcohol with me when she came round – nothing too strong or excessive, you understand, just a glass or two of wine. She always got her partner, Peter, to drop her off and pick her up expressly so she didn't have to drive.

"Oh?" I asked. "You're not driving, are you?" I hadn't seen her car arrive.

"No," she said. "Pete brought me. I've just given it up for a bit."

This was not like her. "Why?" I asked, genuinely puzzled. She didn't drink enough to have to cut down.

"Oh, I'm trying to lose a bit of weight," she said. This was nonsense, and we both knew it. Jenny was maybe half a stone overweight, at most, and had never given a monkey's about looking like a rake. She seemed ashamed, and I tried to hear her thoughts, but there were none. Reddening, I suddenly felt that actively trying to hear someone's thoughts, as opposed to not being able to avoid it, was a betrayal of some kind, so I hastily went out into the kitchen, calling back "Teas all round then!" in a rather too bright and breezy voice.

I brought the tea in and set it on the coffee table. "No biscuits?" asked Jen, naturally enough – usually I'd have provided some sort of munchies with our drink – but then, obviously realising her mistake, "Oh no, I can't have any, I'm dieting."

I looked at her, and I could see she was embarrassed about something, so I moved the conversation on to other topics.

"Peter OK?"

She brightened. "Yeah, he's fine, thanks," she said, evidently grateful for the change. "Just landed a job in Grove Street – you know, by the park. It should take a few months, so he's happy." Peter has his own odd job business, doing building work as well as repairs for local householders. Jen always liked it when his work was close to home.

"Good," I said. "And how's your dad?"

She frowned, and picked up her mug from the table. "Not so good, I'm afraid. He's been harassing the other tenants again." Jen's dad is in his early 70s and has dementia. He lives in sheltered accommodation – Jen's mum died a few years ago, and he had to move out of their house when he couldn't cope on his own. Recently his health had been getting worse and he'd been taking it out on everyone who came his way.

"He's not been hitting them with his newspaper again?" I asked, smiling a little at the thought, though of course it wasn't really funny.

She laughed, but not in a lighthearted way. "No, it's worse than that. Last week Mr Grant, you know, the warden, was round checking on him and dad had a right go at him about the bins. Something to do with where they're kept, or what colour they are – I don't know. He must have been shouting, because his neighbours turned up, wanting to know what was going on, and dad ended up pushing two of them down the hallway. Apparently he was quite violent, and poor Mr Grant ended up with a bruised face from trying to get in-between them."

"Oh dear," I said, picturing the scene. "Did anyone complain?"

"Well, Mr Grant managed to calm everyone down in the end, and he won't be taking it any further – he rang me to tell me, of course, seeing dad is ultimately my responsibility. He was very upset."

"I bet he was. And what about your dad? What did he have to say for himself?"

Jen laughed again, this time more genuinely. "Oh, he blamed everyone else but himself, of course," she said, taking a drink from her mug. "But then there's no change there."

I shrugged. Elderly parents were certainly no laughing matter. As you reached middle age (was 39 middle aged? It certainly felt like it. Since Harry… recently I'd been feeling ancient) and your parents, if you were lucky to still have them, began to get old, they became an extra worry. I was lucky my mum was still healthy and pretty active.

We talked a little about Jen's work, then. She'd been having a few problems with her immediate boss, who for some reason seemed to dislike her, but these appeared to have resolved themselves and she was once more enjoying her job, exhausting though it often was.

I told her about Andrea's visit at the weekend, and how we'd ended up arguing about religion yet again, and she moaned about her brother, who she never saw. "Do you know," she said, "he hasn't been to see dad once since he moved into the flat."

"Not once?" I asked, astonished.

"Not once," she reiterated. "Not even at Christmas."

"Well," I said. "At least Andrea goes to see mum – twice a week, in fact. Wednesdays and Sundays, after church."

Jen smiled. "You could say she goes religiously."

"Indeed."

"And how about you? How are you coping?" Her voice was quiet and gentle.

I didn't want to go there. Other people's sympathy, remember, always made me cry. I flapped a hand at her. "Never mind me," I said, "Tell me more about that hot new doctor."

She looked at me kindly, and I could suddenly hear what she was thinking again: *Poor Steph*, she thought, *I wish I could take it all away.*

That nearly made me cry, so I was glad when she started to describe how Dr Dixon – for that was the hot young doctor's name – had reduced all the female, and a significant proportion of the male, staff to simpering idiots with one look from his gorgeous blue eyes.

"**And** he plays squash," she said, as if this made him the perfect man.

"Of course he does," I said, imagining. Somehow if he'd been a darts player the dream would have been broken. "Does he have a girlfriend?"

"I don't know," Jen said. "And it doesn't really matter, does it? I mean, we're all just fantasising, none of us really want to go out with him."

"Well **you** may be a married woman..."

"We're not married, remember," she said.

"I mean married as in taken," I continued. "But other people may be interested in his current Facebook status."

"Like you, for instance?" she asked, grinning.

"Ah," I said. "I have my own doctor to yearn for." I shocked myself with this, because up until now I hadn't thought I was interested in Dr Reed. Not in that way. Obviously I was…

"Oh yes?" she asked, so I gave her an account of my own dishy doctor. "I think I'll have to invent another illness to go and see him with," I laughed.

Jen raised her eyebrows. "Another?"

"I mean a. Or an. Whatever," I floundered. "Anyway, I need the toilet." And I left the room, silently kicking myself for my blunder.

When I returned Jen was checking her phone. "Everything OK?" I asked, sitting down again.

"Just Pete," she said. "Wants to know what time I want picking up."

"But you only just got here," I said, not unreasonably, I thought.

"Oh no, I'm not going just yet. It's just… he's got an early morning, and doesn't want to be up late." I must have looked puzzled, for she went on: "I think he's got a delivery coming in at seven, or some ungodly hour." She was a lousy liar, and I knew she was making this up. No-one in the building trade works that early.

"Oh, right," I said. This was a bit odd. No alcohol, needing to go home early. What could be going on? I wished she'd just tell me if there was something wrong.

Well she did tell me, though she didn't mean to.

An hour and a bit later, as she was preparing to leave, I was giving her a hug goodbye when I heard her thinking. It shocked me so much I nearly said something, though of course I couldn't. I just pulled away and looked at her, amazed, surprised and, I must say, rather jealous.

I wish I could tell you, Steph, she had thought. *I wish I could tell you about the baby.*

Chapter 11

The next day in work I had a **real** headache, although I didn't think it was a tumour, just stress from having so many cases to deal with. One of our counsellors called in sick, and we had to distribute the clients between us as best we could, so my easing-in period came crashing to the ground.

All day long, as well as the usual strains of dealing with clients' needs, coping with unfamiliar cases and trying to come up with solutions to others' problems, I was forced to listen to people's innermost thoughts as well as their spoken ones, and on more than one occasion had to restrain myself from commenting on what they were thinking rather than saying.

Three times I came to the end of a session and, once the door had closed behind the retreating clients, I sat down at my desk, head in hands, and gave way to tears. My eyes were red, I knew, but there was little I could do about that. There was no way I was going to let people down by giving up – and anyway, clients barely noticed me, I was sure; they were far too busy worrying about their own troubles to notice anyone else.

After lunch (a soggy home-made tuna sandwich at my desk, in case you're wondering) I saw Mrs Harrison, a middle-aged lady with chronic OCD whose life had been put on hold since she developed the condition. I had seen her several times before and we had made a little progress, but not much. She still spent more than six hours a day cleaning her already immaculate house.

"Mrs Harrison, please sit down. How are you today?"

"Oh, not bad, you know?" she said. She had this annoying habit of making nearly every sentence sound like a question, just like many Australians do, and it drove me to distraction. It was like she was questioning the universe. Maybe she was.

"How is the programme coming along?" I asked, as she heaved her not inconsiderable backside into the chair, which always seemed too small for her.

"The programme?" Well at least that **was** a question.

"Yes," I said. "You remember I asked you to try and think about three specific things other than cleaning every day? You were going to write them down."

"Oh that," she said, putting her handbag on the floor and unbuttoning her coat but not taking it off. She was, naturally, immaculately dressed, in quite stylish new clothes. I swear she had a different outfit on every time she came. Maybe she was one of those women who never wore the same thing more than once.

"Yes, the programme," I repeated, as she appeared to have come to a stop. I sat down facing her, and looked over her notes. "Three things every day that don't involve cleaning."

"Well I started?"

"That's good." I had to be positive, even though it was sometimes difficult. "And how far did you get?"

"Well, I thought about two things on the first day – I can't remember what they were, but they weren't cleaning?" I don't know if they were or not, I thought – you tell me.

"And the second day?"

"I can't remember." *Cleaned the fridge* was what I heard in my head.

I nodded. "OK, so you essentially gave up on the programme after the first day. Can you tell me why you did that?"

Mrs Harrison looked sheepish. "I just felt overwhelmed?"

"By the urge to clean?" It was her turn to nod. She was a woman of many words – many of them upturned, as I said – but these diminished to a naughty schoolgirl's mumblings when she considered I was telling her off.

"Is your husband helping you, as I suggested he should?"

"Not really..." she started. *Not at all*, I heard.

"Why not? Did you ask him to?"

She looked ashamed again. "I didn't want him to worry, he has so much on his plate, what with work and all?" Mrs Harrison's husband was ten years older than her, but still worked long hours as a financial adviser. He certainly brought the money in, judging by the descriptions of the large house she gave, but from what I could gather he didn't offer much in the means of emotional support or affection. I had told her I thought she needed to spend more time with him, to get out more, to take up a hobby – anything to take her mind off her obsession with cleaning the house.

"I understand," I said. "But he does have the weekends off, right? And he can surely spare you some time then."

She shook her head sadly. "He has his golf, and his fishing, and he goes to the pub every Sunday afternoon." Does he now, I thought. No wonder you're obsessed with bleach. It was to wash your misery away, wasn't it? The cleaning was there to fill your empty little life with.

"Maybe he'd come in with you next time you're here?" I asked.

She looked aghast, as if I'd asked her to partake in a threesome. "Oh I don't think he'd be able to take time off work," she said. Of course not, I thought. This was all beginning to get me down, and I suddenly felt close to tears again.

"Would you let me ring him?" I asked, not hopeful at all, but running out of ideas.

She shook her head again. "No use," she said sadly. "No use." She looked, then, all of her 53 years, as grey, careworn and used up as an old dishcloth. I felt so sorry for her – then wondered, vaguely, if I myself would be like her in 14 years' time; alone, lonely, searching for meaning in my life. Hell, I was nearly there now!

"Well," I said, "maybe we can continue exploring the reasons behind your OCD." She shifted uncomfortably on her chair. She didn't like talking about her past, I knew from previous sessions, but I felt it was the key to unlocking why she acted like she did – apart from the unfeeling absent husband, which was obviously not helping matters.

As she remained silent, I went on: "We've talked before about your childhood, about how you were always punished for getting dirty, and about how your mother was a…" I looked at my notes. "A fusspot?" she said. I wasn't sure if that was meant to be a question or not, but I answered it anyway. "Yes, a fusspot. She never worked, did she?"

"No. Dad was a plumber, and in those days you didn't work if your husband did. She had four children to bring up – I was the eldest – and that took up most of her time. That, and keeping the house tidy."

Ah yes, of course. Brought up in a household where 'cleanliness was next to Godliness,' where if you got your clothes muddy or ripped you were smacked, and where daddy was absent most of the time would turn anyone a bit fussy, I thought. But I knew there was something else. Plenty of people had an upbringing like that and went on to live normal chaotic lives. There had to have been a trigger.

"Remind me," I said, "when did you start having the urge to clean all the time?"

Mrs Harrison shifted in her seat again. "I suppose it was about 20 years ago?"

"And what was happening in your life back then – you were married, yes?"

"We've been married for 27 years," she said.

"And you weren't working?"

"Never have." *Never wanted to*, came the thought.

"And Mr Harrison... he was in the same job?"

"He's worked his way up from the bottom. He's a hard worker, always wanted to provide for his family?"

His family... "You never had any children, did you?" I asked this last question gently, because although she had told me before that she had no children, I had my suspicions. I knew she didn't have children now, but earlier?

Sure enough, I heard here then – her thoughts, choking and broken, but there: *Only my Aaron. Oh Aaron. Oh*. She looked away, and was silent.

"Mrs Harrison? I know it may be painful, but we need to get to the bottom of your issues. Did you have a child?"

She started to cry, silently, big tears trickling down her worn, tired face and dripping onto her expensive Debenhams skirt. In these situations I just had to let clients cry as long as they needed. I pushed the tissue box across the table towards her, and she silently took one and started dabbing at her tears.

About five minutes later she composed herself enough to talk. And once she'd started she couldn't stop. And you know what? Not once did she use that questioning inflection.

"I only got pregnant once. Oh we tried many times... many, many times, for years, but I only had one pregnancy. Terry was over the moon. He's older than me, as you know, and he had always wanted children. I was made up, too – we'd been married for six years, and were starting to worry it'd never happen. The doctors were no use back then – they didn't have all the tests and treatments they do nowadays, they just let you get on with it. So once I was pregnant we were so careful – Terry wouldn't let me do anything, I had to rest all the time, he did all the housework and everything.

"And when Aaron was born we were both overjoyed. We were a family! I was one of four, as you know, and Terry has two brothers, so we were both so pleased to have started a family at last. It made us complete." I nodded, understanding.

"Terry decorated the nursery. It was light blue, like the sky, with teddy bears stencilled all round the top and a beautiful cot and new furniture and everything. It was lovely. But he only saw it for four days." She stopped then, fresh tears falling, and I urged her to go on if she could.

"I woke up that morning and I just knew something was wrong. I'd slept all night – Aaron hadn't woken me up, like he usually did. My first thought when I opened my eyes and saw it was daylight was: He's dead. And I was right."

Oh I'm so sorry. Struggling to keep my own tears back, I asked her if they knew what it was that 'took him away.'

"Oh they didn't have a clue. Cot death, of course – that's what they'd call it now. Unexplained cot death. Not unusual. Happens all the time."

"I know. More often than you think," I said.

She went quiet then, and I decided to probe her further. "Did you blame yourself? Many mothers whose children die blame themselves. It's a natural reaction." I know this first-hand, I thought.

She looked across at me with red eyes. "Of course I blamed myself. It was my fault. The house must have been dirty."

"Oh no, really, I don't believe that for a minute, and there's no evidence to suggest a spotless house stops cot death. In fact they believe the opposite may well be true. Babies need exposure to some bacteria in order to build up a healthy immune system."

But she just looked at me, all wet eyes and guilt and misery.

"It was my fault. The house was dirty. And I've been cleaning it ever since."

Chapter 12

I had a few such revelations that week at work. It made me realise my new 'gift' may actually be useful – that it may at the very least help me help people help themselves, if that makes sense. (Note to self: look up 'help' in the thesaurus for alternatives.)

On Thursday I had a client with acute zoophobia, or fear of animals. It affected his life so much he could hardly get out of the house, in case he came across a dog or cat. He was frightened of every animal possible, including insects (which is pretty common, I have to say), spiders (again not unheard of) and fish (unusual, but not without precedent).

He'd been coming to me for six months or so on a monthly basis, but we'd never got to the bottom of why he hated anything non-human so much. He talked freely about his childhood, which seemed pretty normal, and his life up to that point – he was in his 30s – but we had never uncovered the cause of his phobia.

That is, until I heard his thoughts as we were discussing how to proceed next. I had just outlined some new treatments which included gradual exposure to the cause of a phobia, in controlled conditions, but told him this would have to be carried out in a different centre to ours and at additional cost – which I knew he could ill afford, being unemployed – when I heard him swearing in his head: *Fucking bastard. Fucking bastard. Fucking Paul.*

Intrigued but cautious, I made a mental note to probe this reference the next time we met – our time was nearly at an end, and I could hardly bring up something so specific without revealing where I'd heard it.

Two sessions later, after much prodding and delving into his childhood (most phobias stem from childhood, so I felt it was a safe bet the cursed Paul was present then) he finally told me how his brother – Paul of course – had sexually abused him at a very young age. The first time it happened he had been watching a documentary about animal life in the jungle.

He had guessed for a long time where his phobia had stemmed from, but had been too embarrassed (and protective of his brother, who he still kept in touch with) to tell anyone.

And that was just one example. Oh it didn't happen every time, of course – not everyone knew where their problems arose from, for a start. And naturally, not everyone happened to think about the right things when I was asking them questions. I heard tons more irrelevant stuff than not. However, I reckoned that if I managed to help even one person gain a better life from hearing what they were thinking, it would be worth all the extra hassle I was going through.

Besides, I was actually beginning to learn how to control my thought-reading, up to a point. The normal everyday babble of thoughts had faded into the background and was bearable, like when you live by a motorway and your brain blocks out the sound of traffic unless you actively think about it. It was when I was close to someone – that is, physically in the same room as them – that I could start to focus on their thoughts if I chose. If not, I could consign it to the background and concentrate on what was being said instead.

So it was with a growing sense of relief and optimism for my continuing sanity that I headed into the third month back at work. Not that everything was rosy again, of course. How could it be? I still felt, every morning after I woke up and, for a split second – oh cruellest of cruelties – thought Harry's death had been a dream, that life was not worth living any more, but as the day went on and I kept on breathing and eating and walking and talking, because I had to... well, life went on, as it does, even after the most crushing of tragedies.

One Sunday I was out walking in the park, as usual. It was a nice sunny day in summer, when the breeze rustled the leaves in the trees and everything seemed bright and clean. No-one could be down-hearted on a day like that, although I couldn't help imagining Harry skipping along in front of me, stopping to chase every pigeon and duck that crossed his path, picking up sticks and throwing stones into the pond.

I was musing on the impossibility of understanding life – indeed, the futility of even trying – when I saw the delectable Dr Reed up ahead, coming my way, being dragged along by a huge Alsatian dog.

Instantly I mentally checked myself over – was I presentable? Well, hardly. I was wearing scruffy torn jeans, a worn and nearly see-through old Pink Floyd t-shirt, and trainers with holes in. I was hardly Amal Clooney. My roots desperately needed dyeing, and my hair hadn't been washed in a week. I suddenly felt decidedly like a bag lady.

Nevertheless, there was no avoiding meeting the doctor. We were on the same path, and unless I actively turned around and headed back the way I had come, we were going to bump into each other. It was just tough I wasn't looking my best.

He too, I was glad to see when he got nearer, was looking less than sartorially elegant, dressed as he was in grubby jeans, baseball boots and a white t-shirt with, I was heartened to see, a hole in the sleeve. His dark brown, wavy hair was messy, as if he hadn't combed it that day, and his chin was darkened by a day-old stubble.

He stopped when he got to within a few feet of me, although the dog was eager to go on, pulling on its lead and sniffing in the direction of a passing pigeon.

"Hello, doctor," I said, bending down to pat his dog. "Is he friendly?" Dr Reed, looking, I have to say, a bit harassed, replied: "She's OK with strangers, unless you happen to have a cat with you, in which case she'll rip your arm off."

I laughed. "**She** looks like she's taking **you** for a walk, not the other way round," I said, stroking her ears as she turned her enormous head round to sniff my crotch. Why are dogs so embarrassing in that way? I gently pushed her head away from my lady bits and tried to tickle her under the chin, but she was having none of it, pulling away again – in search of fresh meat, presumably.

The doctor, struggling to get her under control, said: "You'll have to excuse her. She's my mum's dog, only mum never really got the hang of training and now she's too old."

"The dog or your mum?" I asked.

"Both," said the doctor, and I laughed again. Dr Reed smiled, and I heard him thinking: *Just ask her out, stupid.* Taken aback, I blushed and mumbled something about letting him get on with his walk.

"Yes, yes... I'd better get this one back to mum's for her daily worm dose."

"The dog or your mum?" I asked again, and this time **he** laughed, a deep, dark and dirty laugh which made me feel weird inside. Oh my, I thought, I'd like to hear that laugh in my bed. Not that much laughing has ever gone on in my bed, but you know what I mean. Or if you don't, I feel sorry for you.

The doctor looked at me, smiled, and was about to be dragged off by the dog when I stopped him. "What's your name, by the way?" I asked. "I can't keep on calling you Dr Reed if we're on meeting-in-the-park terms."

He managed to shout it back to me as the Alsatian lunged after a passing duck: "William – but my friends call me Will."

"Will it is, then," I shouted after him, before continuing my walk along the path. Somehow the sun seemed to shine a little brighter as I walked home.

When I got in there was a message on my answerphone from Jenny. We hadn't spoken for a few days, and of course I had kept quiet about the baby – she would tell me in her own time. Eventually she'd have no choice anyway.

After the 'beep' she said: "Hi Steph, it's Jenny. Just wondering if you'd like to go out for a meal next week sometime. I.. er, I have some news... It's good news, so don't you go worrying... er, anyway, hope you get this message. Ring me when you get in. Bye."

Why was it so difficult to leave a coherent message on anyone's answerphone? I smiled to myself – oh, I knew what the news was, of course. I suppose Jenny thought I'd be upset at her having a baby, but this wasn't the case at all. I was made up for her and Pete, and excited at the prospect of having a little one to gurgle at again. I loved babies – loved their tiny hands and feet, their cute little noses, the noises they make (not the crying, obviously).

Harry had been such a perfect baby. He hardly ever cried, only woke up a couple of times at night at most, and spent most of his small and insignificant life laughing and smiling. It was nice to think he never went through anything bad, was never disappointed, never got too upset with life, never had to cope with being dumped by a girlfriend or losing anyone he loved. Those thoughts kept me sane at night.

As I picked up the phone to ring Jenny, the cat came through the door and meowed at me. *Food*, he thought, clear as day.

"OK, Jess, I'm coming," I said, and put the phone down. Jenny could wait til later.

Chapter 13

I remember that Monday in August very well. The weekend preceding it had been really bad. I had spent most of it in bed, sobbing uncontrollably.

This had taken me by surprise, somewhat. I suppose I thought I'd got over the initial period of grief – it had been nearly five months since Harry's tragic death – but of course that was nowhere near true. I'd merely been kidding myself.

Oh sure, I had good days, when the sun was shining and life seemed bearable, at least. When I managed to get through the day without crying. When I ate enough, and actually enjoyed what I was eating. When I laughed, although every laugh seemed like a betrayal in those days.

But that weekend had been different. It was almost like going back to the worst times – the first few weeks after my little boy disappeared from this earth.

The first day I could barely lift my head from the pillow. I only got out of bed to go to the toilet, and that was only because I knew I'd wet the sheets if I stayed there. I didn't eat a thing, and only drank what water I could manage to cup into my hand from the tap.

The cat kept coming into the bedroom and crying for food, or to go out, or whatever – I refused to even listen to his thoughts, poor Jess. In the end he went away and left me to it. When I finally got up, on the Sunday morning, and crawled weakly downstairs I found a neat pile of cat poo by the back door. It stank to high heaven, but I ignored it, automatically put some food in Jess's bowl – much to his relief; he must have been starving – and then went back to bed again.

Later that day I was sitting on the edge of Harry's bed, not sure how I'd got there. I hadn't so much as touched his room since he died, and everything was just as it was on the morning he left it for the last time, if a little dustier.

There were even some dirty clothes flung in a corner – I'd got him a washing basket, but he had never used it, of course. I supposed I'd have to throw them out now.

I picked up one of his favourite cuddly toys – it was a panda he had called Pirate for some reason – and clutched it to my chest, before lying down on his crumpled bedclothes and closing my eyes. There were no more tears left in my body, apparently, so I just dry-sobbed for some time before sleeping once more.

That was a dark weekend.

On the Monday following, I emerged from my bedroom red-eyed and with a blocked-up nose, but managed to get dressed and ready for work. I think I was on auto-pilot. I couldn't face the bus – it was bad enough at the best of times – so I indulged in a taxi, arriving at the office ten minutes early.

In the staff room, one of my colleagues, Sarah, was making a cup of tea. She turned as I walked in, and I could see she was shocked at my appearance, although she tried to hide it.

"Oh, hi Steph," she said, in an unusually high-pitched tone. I grunted at her. "Want a coffee?" I nodded, and sat down at the small table. I stared at the wall, where there were notices about health and safety, confidentiality, safeguarding and all sorts of stuff we needed to know in our job.

A couple of minutes later she placed a mug of hot coffee in front of me, and sat opposite. I could feel her looking at my haggard face, my untidy clothes and my red eyes.

I thought for a minute she was going to comment on how I looked, but instead she started telling me about something her boyfriend had done at the weekend. I wasn't listening, to be honest. I sipped my coffee until she suddenly got up in a rush, looked at her watch, and with a bright "Anyway, I've got a nine fifteen, with someone who really doesn't like me being late, so I'll have to dash!" out the door she went.

We were only a small team. Just the boss, Gary, and four other counsellors including myself, plus an admin guy, Tom, who also acted as a receptionist. Two of the counsellors were part-time in those days, so there weren't usually many people around.

I knew I didn't have an appointment until ten o'clock, so I walked slowly to my office to try and work up some enthusiasm for what I had to get through that day.

My room was a bright one, with a small window which faced the street, and the light hit me as I entered. It was another sunny day outside – this summer had been an unusual one, in that we'd had more than our usual four days of warm weather.

My eyes were still sore from all the crying I had done recently, and I made a mental note to go out at lunchtime and buy some eye drops. Maybe that would make me feel better.

My first client arrived on time, which was unusual for them. It was an elderly man called John Thomas (I often allowed myself an inward, childish chuckle at his name), who had been referred to us by his GP for alcoholism. I knew we were onto a loser with him – after all, he was nearly 80, and had been drinking since he could remember – but we got along OK, and I think he enjoyed talking about the old days.

I wasn't really in the mood to listen to his tales that day, but the session went alright, I managed to speak coherently and I don't think he even noticed my lack of interest. I could hear his thoughts, but they were mainly centred on what he was telling me, so they were neither help nor hindrance.

My second client wasn't until the afternoon – it was a quiet day, appointments-wise – so I spent some time writing reports before lunchtime. I managed to avoid everyone else, sneaked out of the building, nodding to Tom on the desk, and walked up the road to the local shops, where I bought some painkillers for my growing headache and 'rejuvenating' eye drops from the chemist. I wasn't hungry, despite barely eating all weekend, but automatically went to the bakery for a sandwich and a bottle of orange juice. Maybe I'd eat later. Maybe I'd never eat again.

Back in my office I sat staring at the wall until it was time for my next clients. Our offices are painted a soothing lilac colour, and have pretty prints of birds and flowers hanging up. These are supposed to create a calm, relaxing environment. I think they work to some extent.

I was startled from my staring by the desk phone ringing. I snatched it up and Tom's voice told me my clients had arrived. I glanced at the clock on the wall, and was amazed to see it was ten past two. They were late, but I hadn't even noticed.

A minute or two later, without knocking, in walked Stuart and Susan McDonough, the scruffy divorcing couple with two children who I had seen once before. Gary had been looking after them since, but it was Gary's day off, so it was just my luck to get them on a day when I was barely able to function.

I remembered reading their notes, in which Gary had repeatedly written about the husband's barely-concealed hostility and the wife's submissiveness and inability to concede the marriage was finished. Their main worry though, and the reason they were having counselling, was that both of them were demanding custody of their small boys, and neither of them was willing to give an inch.

As soon as they walked in, Susan looking almost as bad as I did, I could hear the husband's thoughts, angry and boiling like a pressure cooker about to explode. *Oh good grief*, I thought, *I could really do without this today*. But there was no way of getting out of it now.

Chapter 14

I started by saying hello, and muttering about how I hoped they were finding these sessions beneficial (*Yeah, right,* I heard Stuart think), and waffling about Gary having filled me in about their situation and other general stuff, before asking them how they had been getting on with the custody issue.

Stuart immediately started a long, sweary rant about how no-one in authority ever listened to him, and how he was never in a million years going to leave his children with that useless bitch, whatever anyone said.

Well, I thought, *this is going to be fun.*

"I assume your social worker, Miss Hancock, has been dealing with that?" I asked.

Stuart grunted, but his wife looked at me with a tearful expression. Even in my somewhat distracted state I noticed she had dark patches under her eyes and a haunted look which made me think of a mouse our cat had brought into the house once. The mouse was in a corner, literally and metaphorically, and Jess was playing with it, hitting it with his paw and jumping on it if it moved too far away. I'd been unable to get it away from its tormentor in time, and its end had not been pretty. It had distressed me for weeks.

I shook my head to clear it, as Susan was saying something I hadn't caught the beginning of.

"…and Miss Hancock said if we went to court it'd take ages, and we don't want that, and we might have to pay, cos they don't always pay these days, what with the cost-cutting an' all, and we don't have any money. I mean, I had to go to the food bank last week, cos Stu can't find a job, and…"

Her husband cut her short by jumping up out of his chair. He startled me, and her, too – she looked shocked, at any rate – and I was about to ask what he was doing when he stormed across the room to the window and stared out of it.

"How the fuck can I get a job when everyone's against me?" he shouted at the people passing by outside.

I glanced at Susan, who was clearly trembling with fear, and gave her a weak smile, which she didn't return.

"Mr McDonough," I said, calmly, "could you come and sit down again, please?"

Stuart turned his head to look at me, and I saw real hatred in his eyes. Hatred of me? Probably not – more like hatred of the world, or his life, or both.

I've learnt from experience that most angry people are really angry at themselves, but they hardly ever admit it, preferring rather to direct their anger at everyone and everything around them. Getting someone like Stuart McDonough to admit they hated themselves was the hardest part of my job.

He continued to glare at me, and I tried to read his thoughts, but they just seemed to be a jumble of rage.

"If you sit down, Mr McDonough," I said, "we can try and find a way around your problems. I know you want us to help you." This was patently untrue, but it was what we normally said to try to get people to co-operate.

Stuart stared a moment longer, then looked at his soon-to-be-ex wife, who was sitting hunched, small and fearful in his presence, which is how I gathered she always was.

"OK," he said, sullenly, shuffling back to his seat and sitting in it heavily. "How can **you** help me, though? I mean, I can't get a job, I have no money, we're behind on the rent, the benefits people are as useful as a pile of shit and my wife wants to take my children away from me. How the fuck are you going to help me, huh?"

"Well," I said, "let me start by seeing if we can find out why you can't get a job. How long have you been unemployed for, Mr McDonough?"

"Three fucking years," he growled.

"OK," I continued, "and in that time I presume you have had help to find a job – gain new skills, get some training, that kind of thing?"

The man stared at me again. "Well, they're a useless bunch of bastards, aren't they?" he asked, angry again.

"Who are, Mr McDonough?" I asked, although I already knew.

"The people at the Job Centre. Ha! Job Centre, that's a laugh, innit? D'you know what they do, Miss, at the Job Centre?" He actually called me Miss, like a schoolboy would. I was probably a few years older than him, no more. I made a mental note that he saw me as a school teacher figure, which may come in useful at a later date.

"What do they do, Mr McDonough?"

He slapped his hand down on my desk, making me jump. "Fuck all, that's what they do! Fuck all! Their only job is to get you off their books – they don't give a shit about my life. They've sent me on the same course three times – three times! – and for what? Nothing, that's what. Absolutely fucking pointless."

I said something about how they are only doing their best in difficult circumstances, and he turned on me again. He sounded less angry this time, more sorry for himself, which is just as damaging. "No, Miss, that's not right. I've got no qualifications – I was never clever, never got school at all, and so there was never any hope for me, was there? And when I got sent down it was the end – there was no going back. Once you've been in prison no-one wants to give you a job, no-one. It's been a fucking nightmare ever since."

Trying to hide the fact I was not remotely surprised no-one wanted to give him a job after he'd spent 18 months in jail for grievous bodily harm – beating up someone unprovoked in the street, apparently – I asked him what jobs he was looking for.

He shrugged, mumbled that he didn't know, but I heard him think: *Gangster. Or drug dealer. Yeah, that'd be good.*

I then turned to his wife, who I knew from looking at her notes had never had a job in her life. She was considerably younger than her husband, but looked older. The years had not been kind to her.

"And how about you, Mrs McDonough? Your boys are both at school now, aren't they? Have you been looking for a job?"

Susan's voice was small, like her: "Well, Ewan's only three, but he's starting pre-school next month. Lucas is going into Year One, he's growing fast."

"And?" I went on.

"And there's no fucking way any wife of mine is going to get a job while the kids are small," her husband interrupted. "It's the man's job to provide for his family. It's **my** job."

Well, you're not doing a very good job of it so far, are you? I wanted to say, but instead: "But your wife may have a better chance

68

of getting a job than you, Mr McDonough, and with the children going into school she'll be able to look for something, even if it's part-time. Surely that would help you with your financial situation?"

"Fuck that," he said, simply, and fell silent.

I felt I was getting nowhere, and although this was not unusual with couples – often one of them wouldn't budge, no matter how much reasoning you did with them – this was an extreme case, and I wasn't really sure how to make any progress at all.

Reluctantly, I asked Mrs McDonough whether they'd made any more decisions about their divorce and custody of the children.

I didn't want to bring it up again when there was so much negativity in the room, but I felt I had no choice. The session was only an hour long, and if they hadn't talked about it at all before the end I would be in trouble with Gary, because that was the issue we were supposed to be helping them with.

The notes told me the pair had agreed to divorce, but were totally divided on who was going to look after their offspring. Still living as a family unit for now, they would be splitting up as soon as they could find somewhere to live apart – council flats, probably. Both of them wanted the children to live with them, and neither would give an inch, even if it was suggested they look after the kids for half a week each.

Social workers had been working hard to get the couple to come to some agreement before the divorce went through, as they were concerned about the children's emotional welfare. Although Stuart had been in prison for violence, there had never been any indication he was capable of hurting his children, so if the case went to the courts they would probably be granted joint residency. Unfortunately, neither of the parents wanted this.

As soon as I brought the matter up, Stuart's hackles raised again.

"They're **my** children," he ranted, "why would I leave them with that simpering, useless woman? She can't even look after herself properly – I mean, look at her. I'm going to have them full-time, and that's that. There's no way any fuckin' snooty-nosed judge is going to take my kids away from me."

Susan sat there silently, and I noticed a single tear trickle from the corner of one eye.

"But surely, for the sake of your children, you must come to some sort of arrangement?" I asked. "They'll want to see both of you, because they love you both." Reminding parents of their children's love usually softened their feelings, but not this time. Stuart glared at his wife and addressed her directly: "You're a useless mother, you know you are. Supid cunt. Just give them to me, I know how to look after them."

I winced at the foul language. I usually let swearing pass, as long as it wasn't directed at anyone else, but I couldn't let this one go.

"Mr McDonough, I can't let you talk to your wife like that when you're in my room," I said, as sternly as I could manage.

The man stood up and stamped over to the window again, where he stared out into the street. He didn't apologise. I'd clearly have to work on the teacher thing. He was acting like a toddler after being told off.

To fill the silence, I went on: "You both know that if your case goes to court it is more than likely you will be given joint custody – that the children will share their time between the two of you. Surely that's got to be better for the boys?"

The couple stayed silent.

I glanced at my notes, and there was a pause while I thought about what to bring up next – there was so much for this couple to resolve, I didn't know where to start.

During the pause – which only lasted seconds – I was shocked to hear a thought coming clearly from Stuart. It made me physically jolt, and I looked up from my notes and stared for a moment at his back, which was all I could see. My blood ran cold, and a chill ran down my spine. There was only blankness, despair and anger in that thought, nothing else.

If I can't have the kids, then nobody else will.

Chapter 15

I thought a lot about that single sentence in the following week. Whatever else I was doing I simply could not get it out of my head. I'd be washing the dishes, or feeding the cat, or walking along the street, when I'd hear those words ringing in my ears, clear as a bell, bleak as the desert: *If I can't have the kids, then nobody else will.*

Stuart McDonough was obviously a damaged man, and potentially dangerous with it. I was worried he may do something to his wife, or even his children, if he didn't get his own way – which of course we all knew he wouldn't, in the end.

But there was very little I could do about it. I couldn't have done much even if he had **said** those words to me; there was bugger all I could do when I'd only **heard** him thinking them.

Desperate to act, even in a small way, I spoke to Gary and asked him to make sure I was the only one who saw the couple in the future. I told him some bull about having built up a small rapport with them (yeah, that was funny, I know), and he believed me. In reality, I just wanted to make sure nothing bad happened.

In addition, I called up the McDonoughs' social worker, Cathy Hancock, and asked her if we could meet to discuss the case. I thought maybe she'd be able to give me some insight into their family life or background, which I could use to probe a little deeper into their situation when I spoke to them next.

Miss Hancock, however, could only fit me in for a meeting in three weeks' time, and warned me she would not be able to discuss anything confidential. Oh great, I thought, but I made the appointment anyway. At least it felt like I was doing something...

In the meantime, I went on seeing my regular clients, as usual, before going home to my now very quiet house every evening, where most days I'd sit and watch TV with a half-eaten microwave dinner on my lap. More often than not, there'd be tears dripping into the curry and rice, but I hardly noticed them anymore.

....

On the Wednesday evening of that week Jenny came round to visit me. I hadn't seen her for ages – we had tried to arrange to go out for a meal since she left the message on my phone, but had not quite managed it. Somehow the meal had turned into a brief home visit, instead.

Of course I knew she was pregnant, but she didn't know I knew. She must be a considerable few weeks along by now, I thought as I opened the door to her – and I couldn't help glancing at her stomach as I greeted her. No, no bump yet.

I think she saw me looking, because she gave me a rather quizzical look, but I ushered her into the living room with a gesture and told her I'd make a cup of tea "because I'm gasping." This wasn't true – I just didn't want her asking anything awkward.

She went and sat down, stroking the cat as he nuzzled her knees. Jess didn't usually like strangers, but he made an exception for Jenny.

When I came into the room a few minutes later bearing two cups of hot tea, he'd made a bold move and was sitting on her lap.

"Oi, Jess," I said, putting the mugs down on the coffee table, "Jenny doesn't want you mauling her, get off." I pushed him gently with my palm, and he issued a faint "meow" in protest, which I heard in my head as a firm "*no.*"

"It's OK, Steph," Jenny said, laughing, "he's OK. It's not often I get some affection."

"Oh dear," I said, mock sympathetically, sitting down on the sofa next to my friend. "Pete's not renowned for his romance, is he?"

Jenny laughed again. It was nice to hear it in my too-quiet house. "Oh I didn't mean that," she said.

We talked about work, Jenny's dad, and a documentary we both saw on television the night before, for quite some time before I realised she'd stopped talking. I knew she wanted to tell me something – presumably about being pregnant – but I couldn't hear her thinking anything at all.

"Well," I said in the end, after a short silence. "I've got nothing else to tell you about really – life's very boring these days." This was untrue, as you know, but I could hardly tell anyone why.

Jenny sighed, then put her hand on her stomach – the cat had by this time got tired of his new friend and gone upstairs to bed – and I suddenly knew what she was going to say, thought-reading aside.

"I've got something to tell you, Steph," she said, and there was a catch in her voice.

"Oh yes?" I replied, trying to sound all innocent and unknowing, and failing. Steph looked at me, sitting by her side, and smiled.

"You already know, don't you?" she asked. There was puzzlement in her voice as well as amusement.

I grinned. "You're having a baby," I blurted out. I think I sounded pleased, because I was.

Steph surprised me by bursting into tears, while nodding furiously.

Somewhat shocked, I went to get her a tissue from the kitchen, but by the time I returned she had recovered her composure a little and was smiling, if a little damp.

"That's great news!" I enthused. "Really, Jen. It's about time!"

She laughed, took the tissue I offered her and wiped her eyes. "I wanted to tell you ages ago," she started, "but… well, with your loss, and all, and…"

"It's OK, really," I said. And it was. "I'm so pleased for you. How far gone are you?"

"Oh, about 16 weeks," she said, patting her still almost normal-looking stomach. "I knew I might start showing soon, and I didn't want you to see a bump before I told you."

"Wow," I said, staring at her as if she'd suddenly grown another head, which in a way she had.

Jenny sniffed, and blew her nose. "How did you know, anyway?"

I hesitated. Could I tell my best friend my biggest secret? Was this the moment I told someone for the first time?

No. And no.

"Erm.." I faltered, "I just guessed. You know, the not drinking, the early nights, the lack of enthusiasm for the pub…" I laughed, uncertain that she'd believe me. But in the end, what else could it have been?

"Of course," she said, smiling again.

We spent the rest of the evening talking babies, specifically how Pete was going to cope with a newborn ("He can just about look after himself. He'll be useless," was Jenny's rather unfair assessment), how long the new mum was planning to have off on maternity leave ("As long as they'll let me"), and about the need to get to know other new mums.

"The best thing I did when I was pregnant," I told her, "was make friends with other mums at the antenatal classes. You really need someone who's going through the same experience as you – nobody else understands what it's like. Even people who've already had babies forget.

"And then after the babies are born, you have some ready-made babysitters and playmates for your kid when it's grown a little. It's a win-win situation."

"OK, I'll make a note," said my friend, looking at her watch. "Anyway, Pete's coming to pick me up soon. Early night, and all that."

"You on an early shift tomorrow?" I asked.

Jenny shook her head. "Afternoon. Which means I get a nice lie-in."

"Good for you," I said.

Her phone made a sudden noise like a duck, which was her text alert. She read the message and tutted. "It's Pete. He's outside, says he won't come in. I'll have to go."

"You got anyone interesting coming in this week?" she asked as she stood up.

I started a little. "Well, now you know I can't talk about my clients – client confidentiality, and all that," I said, a little defensively. It's true in the past I may well have discussed, in a general kind of way, you understand, some of the more amusing aspects of being a counsellor, but I had never gossiped about anyone, never gone into details, and certainly never named names.

Jenny laughed a little uncertainly, and headed out of the room. "I know you can't," she said. "Which is a shame, really – I bet you have some really juicy information on the local nutters."

"They're not nutters," I countered, following her. "Well... most of them aren't. They're just normal people with problems."

We went into the hall and Jenny put her coat on.

As she hugged me goodbye, she suddenly stopped in her tracks and pulled back.

"Oh, there's some news I've been meaning to tell you," she said.

"You already told me you're pregnant," I said, smiling. "I know baby brain can make you forget things, but that's ridiculous."

"Oh ha ha," she laughed mockingly. "No... you remember Dr Reed, who was working as a locum at our doctors?"

How could I forget? I nodded, trying not to appear too interested. "What about him?" I asked, opening the door so my friend could leave.

"He's just got a permanent position at our walk-in centre. I saw him the other day. Everyone's lusting after him."

"Oh," was all I could manage, while my heart sank at the thought of never seeing him again.

Chapter 16

In fact, I saw the luscious Dr Reed just a few days after the evening with Jenny. It was Sunday, and I was walking in the park, getting some much-needed fresh air, when I saw him coming towards me with his mum's huge Alsatian.

This time I was slightly more presentable – I had a new coat on, to keep out the encroaching chill of an unusually cold early autumn, and new trainers, too, although I knew my hair needed washing, as usual.

As he got nearer, I could see how much he was struggling with the dog, and I laughed inwardly. Outwardly, I smiled as he came closer, trying but largely failing to keep the hound in check.

"We'll have to stop meeting like this," he said, laughing as he pulled on the lead, barely making an impression on the dog's progress. We stopped on the pathway, and I patted the Alsatian's massive shoulders.

"She taking you for a walk again?" I asked, pretty unnecessarily, to be fair.

"Yup. Twice round the lake then back home is about all I can manage without having a nervous breakdown," replied the doctor, once more straining to keep his canine charge from running off.

"Mind if I walk with you?" I asked, turning on the spot and facing the way I had just come.

"I'd be honoured," he said, and my heart leapt a little in my chest.

Allowing himself to be dragged once more along the path, Will Reed trotted rather than walked towards the park lake, which this time of the year was teeming with ducks, coots and moorhens, all trying to find shelter from the wind and search for food in the weeds.

Unlike the height of summer, when the park was full of children bearing bags of stale bread to throw at the wildfowl before heading for the playground, the pathways at this time of year were mainly populated by dog-walkers and the odd lonely soul, like myself, with nothing better to do on a Sunday afternoon.

The wind was whistling in the trees, blowing several brightly-coloured leaves to the ground, where they joined a growing pile. Within a couple of minutes we had reached the lake, where the water was being churned up by the breeze and the ducks huddled together for warmth or companionship, or maybe both.

I pulled the zip of my coat up a little higher, as the wind was now blowing directly towards us. My face felt cold, but my body was warm enough.

It was quite difficult to keep pace with my new walking companion – although I always walked quite briskly, he was having to half-run to keep up with his badly-trained doggy friend. I wanted to chat, but knew I couldn't really do so in these circumstances. Whenever I caught up with the pair of them, the words I tried to speak seemed to be blown away by the rising wind and never made it to his ears.

As we reached the end of the lake and started to walk around it to the other side, I was beginning to despair. I knew I liked this man – well, I didn't know him very well, but I certainly found him attractive, and wanted to get to know him better – but fate seemed to be keeping us apart.

Trotting to keep by his side, I resolved that, when we parted as he left to take this monstrous hound back to his mother, I was going to ask him to go for a coffee or drink sometime. I had to do something. I mean, I didn't even know if he had a girlfriend, or even a wife, but I had heard him thinking of asking me out, so it was certainly worth a try.

We rounded the end of the lake and crossed the small, arched wooden bridge which took us over a man-made stream feeding into the main body of water. It was narrow and greasy with moss and fallen leaves, and could be quite treacherous in the autumn months.

As we crossed the bridge my foot slipped and I put out a hand to steady myself. I grabbed Will's arm without thinking, and managed to stop myself from falling flat on my face – unfortunately, the unexpected jolt on his arm made him drop the lead, and both of us watched, appalled, as Will's canine charge saw her chance and ran off down the path, lead trailing behind her, tail wagging madly.

We stopped dead, still on the bridge, shocked. Will turned to look at me, and I immediately started apologising, stumbling over the words in my embarrassment.

The good doctor held up his hand and stopped me with a half-hearted smile. "It's not your fault," he said. "It's OK, she's run off before – she'll probably just race around the park for two hours before going home for dinner. She knows the way – it's only round the corner. But I should try and get her back."

And he quickly started off in the direction the dog had raced, shouting her name: "Mabel! Come on Mabel!"

I ran after him, and, catching him up, rather breathlessly asked: "Mabel? Really?"

He glanced at me, grinned, and shrugged his shoulders. "It's my mum's dog. I didn't choose it." He shouted again: "Mabel! Come on Mabe!" I giggled.

There was no sign of Mabel. By this time she was probably chasing rabbits in the nearby field or harassing the children in the playground. A worrying thought crossed my mind.

"She's not likely to… attack… anyone, is she?" I asked, as we hurried down the path at the opposite side of the lake from where we'd met.

Out of the corner of my eye I saw Will shake his head. "No, thankfully, she's a big old softie, although she can be a bit boisterous… and she hates squirrels, so…"

At that moment a blood-curdling scream assaulted our ears. We stopped in our tracks for the second time, and looked at each other in horror. My first thought was that the big softie Mabel had ripped someone's throat out in an act of boisterousness. I think Will had the same horrifying thought, as his face drained of all colour and his brown eyes were wide.

As one, we started running down the path, in the direction from which the scream had come.

Within a few seconds we could see, on the path up ahead, a small group of people huddled by the side of the lake. My heart sank as we got nearer, and I saw an elderly lady with a small dog on a lead turn away from the group. She seemed to be crying.

Please let it not be Mabel, I begged, as we got closer. Will got to the group ahead of me, and I heard him ask: "What is it? What's the matter?"

Someone mumbled something I didn't catch, and then Will pushed his way through the crowd, calling: "Get back! I'm a doctor! Out of the way!" My heart sank, and my stomach lurched with anticipation, but I pushed my way behind him nonetheless.

What I saw haunted my nightmares for several weeks afterwards. Lying on the cold ground was a small boy – a toddler, no more than two years old. He was lifeless, but dripping wet, his blond hair dark and limp against his pale face, his eyes closed.

Crouching next to him was a young man, in his 20s I guessed, with eyes as wide as saucers and a face as white as a sheet. He was touching the boy's face, and crying silently.

I heard Will, in front of me, shout "Someone call an ambulance," and he grabbed the man by the arms. "What happened? Did he go under the water? Did he bang his head?" His voice was urgent but calm, and the man stared at him, unresponsive. He was obviously in shock. I knew how he felt – I had form.

A middle-aged lady standing next to me stepped forward. "We dragged him out of the water," she said breathlessly. "I don't think he was in there long, maybe a minute, but he hasn't regained consciousness. I don't know if he banged his head." Her voice had a catch in it, and she started crying. The arms of her expensive-looking faun-coloured coat were wet and covered in pond weed.

By this time a man to my left had got through to the ambulance service on his mobile, and I heard him giving the address of the park. Will was examining the boy, looking for a pulse, and then quickly he said: "He's not breathing, so I'm going to give him CPR. Tell the ambulance a doctor is administering CPR."

I heard the man on the phone repeat the message, and then watched, horrified, as Will started breathing into the boy's mouth. The man who was with the lad – his dad, presumably – stood up and looked on, clearly horrified. He was running one hand through his hair in an agitated manner.

Suddenly I couldn't do it anymore. I had to get away. I'm ashamed to say I pushed my way back out of the small crowd of people and staggered down the path to a nearby bench, where I almost collapsed in a sobbing heap.

It was just too upsetting for me to see another little boy lifeless, his tiny body lying on the dirty floor... it reminded me too much of my Harry. I couldn't bear to watch.

After a few minutes I was aware of another person sitting next to me on the bench. I looked up and saw the middle-aged lady who had spoken earlier. She was dabbing her eyes with a tissue, her glasses on her knee.

"Are you OK, love?" she asked.

I nodded, not trusting myself to speak just yet.

The woman sighed, put her glasses back on then continued in a faltering voice: "It's just awful... awful... I've never seen anything so..." she sighed again, and turned to look at the group of people. They were blocking our view to Will and the boy, I was glad to say. I didn't want to see him.

I rubbed my dripping nose with my sleeve, putting snot on my new coat. "What happened?" I asked. It seemed the right thing to say.

The woman picked her glasses off her nose again, and I saw she was shaking. Her coat sleeves were dripping onto her lap, but she didn't seem to notice.

"I don't really know," she said. Her voice was shaking too. "I was just walking along and I heard a scream. I turned around and there was the man – the dad, I think – standing by the lake just behind me. He was screaming, and I looked and saw the little lad, face down, in the water. I ran back, and dragged him out. He was heavy..."

She stopped, and I realised I was crying again.

"I expect he just slipped," she went on. "I mean, the path's full of leaves, they should really clear them up..."

Suddenly she got up, replaced her glasses and set off back to the crowd, which seemed to be growing as more people came along.

"I need to see..." she was saying, as she headed back to where Will was trying to revive the boy. I didn't want her to go.

Left alone, I sat staring at the crowd, eyes blurry, until I heard the ambulance sirens – the park entrance was pretty close; they wouldn't have far to come.

And then, to my eternal shame, I got up, and walked briskly away.

Chapter 17

That had been about three o'clock. By eight I was sitting on my settee, staring at the television – I couldn't concentrate to watch anything; it was just background noise. I had a cup of coffee in my hand, but it had long gone cold and I had barely touched it.

I had little recollection of the intervening hours. I remembered walking home in a daze, eyes blurry with tears, and automatically feeding the cat when I got in. After that? I think I had just sat there, staring.

I wanted to know what happened to the little boy, really I did – I mean, what sort of uncaring person wouldn't? But… but I didn't want to hear bad news, so had avoided putting the local radio or TV news on just in case.

Several times I had thought about contacting Dr Reed, but of course I didn't have his phone number – he wouldn't be at work now – and I had no other means of reaching him. It crossed my mind to ring Jenny, but I didn't want to upset her, especially not 'in her condition,' as they say.

So I just sat there, trying not to think.

Just after eight there was a knock on the door. It startled me so much I spilled some of the cold coffee on my jeans.

"Shit," I said, getting up and placing the cup on the coffee table. "Who the fuck is that?" I didn't want to talk to anyone tonight – except myself, clearly, which was something I was doing more and more.

I opened the door and Will Reed was standing there. For a second I didn't recognise him. His long-ish wavy hair was messy and he looked drained. He was holding a small bunch of flowers.

"I just wanted to see if you were OK," he said.

I stared at him, too startled to say anything just yet. All that was going round my head was the thought: *How does he know where I live?*

"I… Steph? Can I come in?"

I stepped back and gestured for him to enter. He came through the door and stood in the hallway, looking confused.

I tried to pull myself together. "Go in, go in," I said, "don't stand there like a spare part." And I followed him into the living room, where we both sat down awkwardly, him on the only armchair in the room, me on the sofa.

Will seemed to remember the flowers in his hand, for he looked at them then held them out. "These are for you," he said. "They're not very good ones, I admit, as the only shop I could find open was the garage, but they might cheer the place up a bit…"

Silently, I took the small bunch of flowers – I had no idea what they were called, but they were yellow and white – and placed them on the settee next to me. They were wrapped in cheap paper, which was damp at the end. "Thanks," I said absently.

A few silent seconds went by, and then we both spoke at once: "How…" "I…"

Will laughed, and it sort of broke my shock a little. He had such a nice laugh. Deep and genuine.

He gestured for me to go first, waving his hand in my direction.

"How did you know where I live?" I asked.

Will smiled. "I've been here before, remember?" he asked gently.

It took me a few seconds, but I remembered. Will on the end of my bed, gently patting my hand on the day after Harry…

"Yes. Yes, of course," I said hastily, not wanting to recall.

I looked at him, at his dark brown eyes which were staring into mine, so kind and caring, and then looked away.

"I wanted to see if you were alright," he said. "And to let you know the boy is OK."

Something broke in my chest – relief, I suspect – and I burst into tears. Huge sobs racked my body, and I thought for a moment I was having some sort of breakdown, but I couldn't help it.

Within a second Will was sitting next to me, his arm around my shoulders. Uncaring about what he'd think, I turned and sobbed against his chest.

I don't know how long we stayed like that. Probably only a few minutes, though it seemed like longer.

Neither of us said anything. Will just held me, his arms strong, his chest warm, as I cried, tears and snot wetting his rather expensive-looking leather jacket.

After a while I pulled away, suddenly conscious of how I must look. I hunted in my fleece pocket for a tissue, but found none, so got up and went into the kitchen for one. When I returned Will was still sitting on the settee, and he had moved the flowers onto the coffee table and turned the television off.

"I'm sorry," I said through my blocked nose. "I just... well, you know."

"You have nothing to be sorry about," he said. He stood up, and ushered me towards the settee. "Here, sit down, and let me get you something to drink." I half-collapsed on the sofa and dried my eyes with the tissue.

"What do you want? Tea? Coffee? Wine? Gin and tonic? Singapore sling?"

I smiled a little through my tears. "Aren't **I** supposed to make **you** a drink?"

Will picked up the mug containing the cold coffee and turned to me. "It's fine, I know how... actually, do you have any hot chocolate? I make a mean hot chocolate."

I thought for a second. "I think so..."

He smiled. "Hot chocolate it is, then. Mind if I join you?"

Ten minutes later we were sitting side by side in companionable silence, drinking creamy hot chocolate from two of my biggest mugs. I had to use two hands to hold it. It was probably the best hot chocolate I had ever had.

"Go on then," I said at last, sighing. "Tell me what happened." I was ready.

Will sighed too. "It seems the lad slipped while running on the path and fell into the lake," he said. I nodded – this much I already knew. "His dad screamed, and a lady ran back and dragged him out. He was only under for seconds... but he must've taken in a lot of water; I think he went in head-first."

I shivered, and took another sip of my drink.

"Anyway, I gave him mouth-to-mouth and chest compressions, but he didn't respond. The ambulance came pretty quick, and they took over. His dad went with him. I stayed to check everyone else was OK, and then I saw that you had gone."

I grunted. "I just couldn't..." I mumbled.

Will put a hand on my arm. "It's OK, I wasn't criticising. It must have been a shock for you. I wanted to go and find you straight away, but first I had to deal with one of the ladies in the park, who was having a bit of a delayed panic attack, and then I remembered Mabel…"

I started. I'd forgotten about Mabel. "Did you find her?" I asked.

Will put his hot chocolate on the table. It was nearly empty. "Well, it's more accurate to say she found me," he said. "I was walking back to mum's to see if she'd gone home when she came up behind me and nearly knocked me over."

I smiled, picturing it, then frowned. "You said the boy was OK…"

"Yes. Well, he's going to be. I took Mabel home, told mum what had happened, then went home myself to clean up. I left it a while – hospitals are busy places, you know – and then rang to see how the lad was. They said he regained consciousness in the ambulance, that he was breathing on his own and they were pretty certain he'd recover just fine."

"Thank goodness," I breathed. "The poor little mite. It's a good job you were there." I was on the verge of tears again, and I knew it, so I was about to change the subject when my stomach made a loud rumbling noise. Suddenly I was starving.

Will must've heard it, for he said: "Have you eaten?"

I shook my head. I hadn't been hungry until now.

"Neither have I. Do you fancy chips? I do believe the chippy's still open."

I smiled. I hadn't been to the local chip shop in months. Harry and I used to get chicken nuggets and chips with curry sauce every Saturday as a treat. It had made him so happy.

"I'd love chips," I said.

"Chips it is, then," said Will.

Chapter 18

Paradoxically, that evening turned out to be one of the best of my life.

On the face of it, having chip butties and Coke in your own home while chatting about something and nothing with someone you barely know is not up there with viewing the Taj Mahal or watching the sun set on a Caribbean island, but it was special, alright.

At around ten o'clock, all chipped out, Will said he'd have to go home, as he was on a 12-hour shift in the walk-in centre tomorrow and he needed to be fresh. I saw him to the door and he paused, before kissing me on the cheek. I think I blushed.

"See you. Thanks for the chips," I said, as I opened the door.

He paused again, and I heard him thinking: *Just give her your number, stupid.* His inner voice was clear as a bell in my head.

Feeling bold, and more cheerful than I had in a long time, I saved him the bother. "D'you fancy going for a drink sometime?" I asked.

The good doctor grinned his lovely grin. "Well, I don't drink, but we could go for a meal... I mean, that's if you fancy it..."

"It's a date," I said. "Here, let me write my number down..." and I scribbled my mobile number on one of the scraps of paper I kept by the landline phone on the hall table.

I handed it to him, he placed it carefully in his pocket, and then he kissed me again, this time on the lips. It was only a peck, but it made my heart sing.

....

Because of Will's work commitments, it was the end of the week before we could go out for a meal. In the meantime we texted each other every day, about boring stuff – nothing too personal – but my heart still leapt every time my text alert went off.

Even in work I was pretty happy. None of the clients could get me down, not even the McDonough couple – although I admit they seemed to do their best.

I saw them on the Wednesday morning. Although I had asked to be their main counsellor, I almost dreaded their appointments, as I seemed to be getting nowhere fast and I found both of them so upsetting, for different reasons.

This week the pair of them turned up looking worse than ever. Stuart was wearing a torn t-shirt and no jacket, despite the chilly autumn weather, while his wife looked like she'd been dragged through a hedge backwards. Her unwashed hair was tied up in a messy bun, and she was carrying a huge plastic bag which seemed to be full of toys.

They both sat down, and I noticed Stuart immediately move his chair further away from his wife's. He obviously didn't like being close to her.

Most of the session consisted of Stuart criticising everyone in his life – including me at one point – and ranting about how unfair everybody was. It seemed the couple were about to be evicted from their flat, because they hadn't been able to pay the rent for some time, and that although Susan and the two little boys would be given emergency accommodation when that happened, Stuart would probably be homeless.

It was understandable they were both upset, but neither of them seemed capable of taking control of their own lives, or even trying to, and it infuriated me.

"Do you have anyone you can stay with, Mr McDonough? Family or friends who can put you up for a few weeks?" I knew I was clutching at straws, and that this wasn't really my job, but I had to try and help.

The man just glared at me from under his thick brows, and it was his wife who answered. "His ma and da disowned him years ago, his brother's in jail and he doesn't really have any friends… at least, not ones with houses…" She was beginning to cry, and I realised that even though he was usually a total bastard to her, she probably still cared for him.

"Can Miss Hancock not help you at all?" Miss Hancock was the pair's social worker.

"Fucking useless bitch," Stuart spat out, and I winced. He probably talks about me like that behind my back, I thought.

"I'm sure she's doing all she can to help, but you must understand the children are the priority in every situation," I said. "The council has a duty to look after them first and foremost. There are hostels you can go to, short-term."

"Fuck that," came the short reply.

I let the curse pass. I knew, as did Stuart, obviously, that the homeless hostels really were the last resort. Depressing, dangerous and full of depraved and often mentally ill individuals, they were to be avoided at all costs, even for one night. Sleeping on the streets was more preferable for most people.

Hell, if **I** was homeless I'd rather have slept in the park than in any of the hostels I'd seen.

I tried to move the conversation on; after all, they only had an hour with me, and we were supposed to be trying to work through their differences. Yeah, fat chance of that, I thought.

I looked at their notes, and when I glanced up I noticed Mrs McDonough was fiddling with her ring finger. She moved her hand a little, and I saw her wedding ring was gone – there was a definite mark where it had been, but it was no longer there. She saw me looking.

"I sold it," she said shortly. "Only got twenty quid for it – scrap value, the man said."

I stared at her, and she went on: "It's not worth keeping it anymore, anyway – the divorce came through. We're no longer Mr and Mrs." She glanced sideways at her ex-husband, who was staring into space. I tried to read his thoughts, but got nothing.

"Oh, right," I said, a little taken aback. "So should I call you something else then, Mrs… I mean, Susan?"

She laughed a little, though there was little humour in it. "Call me what you like," she said.

I tried to take charge of the discussion again. "How does that make you feel – being divorced, I mean."

She just shrugged, and I heard her former husband thinking *Abso-fucking-lutely pointless.*

What was pointless I didn't find out. Instead, we talked a little about what was going to happen once they were evicted – which seemed to be inevitable – and I tried to get them to agree on how many days Stuart would look after the children once he had found somewhere to live. Of course, if – while – he was homeless he would not be able to look after the children on his own; he would have to visit them at Susan's, wherever that turned out to be.

This appeared to infuriate the man. He embarked on a five-minute rant about how life had never gone his way, how no-one was ever fair to him and how he wished he was dead. He never left his seat, but he kept hitting his knee with his fist, as if he could punch his way out of this situation. His ex-wife looked on, eyes weary – and wary, I noticed.

He paused for breath, and I managed to get a word in. "You have to try and focus on your problems one at a time," I said. "And not think too far ahead. The first thing you need to do is ensure your children are well looked after when – if – you get evicted. Then your next priority is to find yourself somewhere to live, where you can sort yourself out."

Stuart surprised me by suddenly standing up. For a scary moment I thought he was going to hit me, but instead he stormed over to the window and stared out at the autumn gloom. I could hear his thoughts again: *Abso-fucking-lutely pointless. Abso-fucking-lutely pointless.*

Yeah, I thought, I know what you mean, mate. I know what you mean…

At the end of their session I told them I was going to ask if they could have separate sessions from now on. I thought I may make better progress with the pair of them if I saw them alone, although I would have to get the local authority to agree to the funding.

Mrs… Susan agreed lone sessions may be better. In fact she seemed positively cheerful about it, and I was not surprised. Her ex-husband, on the other hand, scowled at me as if I had suggested he cut off his own toes, and asked if he had to come back.

I explained that the sessions were entirely voluntary, but that he would be given more chance of gaining better access to his sons if he showed willing. "The social workers like to see you making an effort to improve," I said.

As the pair left, him not holding the door but letting it fall back on his former wife, who was struggling with the bag of toys, I heard him thinking once again: *Abso-fucking-lutely pointless.*

Chapter 19

The rest of the week wasn't as bad as that Wednesday with the McDonoughs, but by the time it finished I was certainly in need of a night out.

Will wasn't working on Friday or Saturday, so we settled for Friday night for our first proper date. He booked a table at an Italian restaurant in town, and told me he'd pick me up at 6.30.

I was nervous as hell, but excited, too. This would be the first date I'd been on since I split up with Gerry, and I didn't want to even think about how long ago **that** was. While I had Harry to look after, the thought of starting a new relationship had somehow never even crossed my mind.

I spent the limited time I had after arriving home from work fussing about getting ready. I didn't have many clothes – most of my money had gone on stuff for Harry – so the choice was limited, but I managed to try four different outfits on nonetheless. I wasn't happy with any of them, really, but settled for black leggings, black boots and a loose flowery top I judged made me look less frumpy than the other choices. I'd lost quite a bit of weight in the last six months or so – most of it unintentional – and I thought I was now too skinny.

My hair had been washed the day before, and I never usually styled it – brush and go was my hair-care motto – but I decided to get the little-used straighteners out of the cupboard and force the wavier strands into some semblance of order. I was moderately pleased with the result.

As for make-up, well… that has always been a bit of a mystery to me. I'd never worn more than a touch of eyeliner and lipstick when I was younger, and now… suffice to say I decided leaving well alone was the better option. Besides, the few bits of make-up I still owned were older than some of my friends, so were perhaps best thrown in the bin. I think I kept them for old time's sake.

When the doorbell went at precisely 6.30 – so he was punctual, then – I hastily sprayed myself with Eau de Polecat, or whatever the hell it was called, and almost ran to the door.

Will was wearing smart jeans, black boots and the same black leather jacket he'd had on when we last met. His hair was tidier than normal, and he smelt nice – I think he'd made an effort too.

I smiled at him. "Hi!" I said. "Are you coming in, or shall we go straight there?"

"Straight there, I think," said the doctor. "I booked the table for seven, and it's always a bugger to park round there." I closed and locked the door, and followed him down the path. His car, parked just a few houses down, was an old-ish, small, two-door saloon – don't ask me what make, I'm not a car person. It was black – that I do know.

He opened the door for me and I climbed in. Inside was clean and tidy. I'd never had a car myself (I'm ashamed to say I can't drive), and most of my automotive experience consisted of reluctantly sitting in Gerry's dirty old banger of a Ford, which had been full of empty crisp packets and pieces of paper. This, by comparison, was the height of luxury.

"Nice," I commented, as I buckled up my seatbelt. Will glanced at me sideways from the driver's seat. "You think?" he asked quizzically.

I looked around. The back seat was totally devoid of smelly McDonald's wrappers. "Yep," I said.

Will shrugged and drove us the three miles or so to the centre of town. We chatted as we went – about the weather, which had been appalling recently, and how busy the walk-in centre was that week.

Amazingly, we found a parking space in a one-way street behind the big supermarket, and made it to the restaurant with ten minutes to spare. Thankfully, they already had our table ready – I hate waiting – so we went and sat down. The restaurant was quite full, and they put us on a tiny two-person table at the back, close to the door leading to the kitchen.

It was a bit gloomy, and obviously not the best table in the house, but I didn't care.

"I'm famished," I said as I read the menu. "I only had a tuna sandwich for lunch, and that was about midday."

"What do you fancy?" asked Will. I smiled to myself. *You*, I thought, but of course I didn't say it. "Erm… pasta, I suppose."

"Think I'll have the spaghetti carbonara," he said after a minute or two. "I've had it before and it's really authentic."

"Oh, I can't have spaghetti in a restaurant," I said.

Will looked up from the menu. "Why not?"

I laughed, embarrassed. "I have to eat it with a knife and fork."

"Well, I'm sure they'll give you cutlery…"

"No, I mean I can't eat it with a fork and spoon, like the Italians do. I only have a small mouth, and that way makes the mouthfuls too big."

I realised I was beginning to sound deranged, but had to go on explaining: "Years ago Gerry and I were in an Italian restaurant, and I was happily eating my spaghetti my own way, when the owner – I believe he was actually Italian – interrupted my meal and humiliated me in front of the entire restaurant by giving me a lesson in how to eat."

Will laughed. "I've never eaten spaghetti in a restaurant since," I finished, blushing, and went back to the menu.

"Oh, well maybe I'll have pizza instead," said Will.

"**You** can have what you like. I expect you're an expert with the spoon method," I said hurriedly. "Pizza always confuses me when I'm out – are you supposed to eat it with your fingers?"

Will turned the page over. "They do a mean calzone," he suggested.

I shook my head. "Too big," I said. Will sighed – a small, almost silent sigh, but a sigh nonetheless. I nearly kicked myself under the table. I knew I was being awkward. I was just so nervous, and out of practice at this sort of thing.

Suddenly I slammed the menu shut with an audible slap. "Lasagne," I said shortly. "No-one objects if you use a knife."

At that moment the waitress came back and took our order. Will went for the spaghetti, as planned. When I asked for a glass of white house wine, the waitress asked if we wanted a bottle. I said yes – but Will interrupted me. "Just tap water for me, please," he said to the waitress.

When she'd gone, taking the menus with her, he continued, rather apologetically: "I don't drink alcohol."

"Oh," I said. I admit I was rather taken aback. I didn't meet many people who were teetotal. "What, not at all?" I asked.

Will shook his head, and fiddled with the knife in front of him. "It's a long story," he said. He sounded a bit upset, so I tried to change the subject.

"Have you been here before?" I knew the restaurant had been open for some years, although I had never eaten there. Gerry and I used to go to one closer to home.

Will looked at me from under his brows. "Not for some time," he said. "My... wife... and I used to come here before it changed hands. It was nice."

I was shocked, and my stomach lurched. His wife? I sort of assumed he was single. Maybe I shouldn't have done.

I think my jaw dropped a little, because Will smiled a sad sort of smile and went on: "It's OK, I'm not married. My wife died nearly three years ago."

"Oh," I said, and then, for want of anything better to say, "I'm sorry."

Will stared at me. "Why?" he said. He sounded annoyed.

"Wh.. why what?" I asked, quite defensively.

"Why are you sorry? What are you sorry for? Did you have anything to do with my wife's death?"

This was getting ridiculous. This was not the dream first date I had imagined. "Of course I didn't. I don't – didn't – even know her. Until two seconds ago I didn't even know she existed, which, to be honest, I'm quite annoyed about. I only meant I'm sorry to hear that... sorry she's dead."

This didn't seem to help. Will was still angry. "Are you?" he asked. "If she were still alive you wouldn't be here now, would you? So why are you sorry?"

While I was staring at him, dumbfounded, the waitress brought our drinks on a tray.

"A white wine for you, madam, and a jug of tap water for you, sir. Enjoy." And she left.

We sat in silence for what must've been a minute. I sipped my wine, too aware that Will was teetotal, and was probably judging me, and searched my memory for something I may have said or did which had got us to this awkward place so early in the evening. I glanced at my watch. It was only 7.20. So far the date was going swimmingly, I thought.

Suddenly I heard Will's voice in my head: *You idiot. You fucking idiot.*

I didn't know who he meant, him or me, so I tried to say something: "I didn't mean to upset you," I started, but he interrupted me. "No, no, **I'm** sorry," he said. "It's just I hate it when people say they're sorry when they hear bad news."

"O..K.." I faltered, wondering what else he expected them to say.

He looked into my eyes and smiled, and I saw the warmth return to his features. "Let me explain…" I nodded for him to go on. "Whenever I tell people about Mia – her name was Mia – they always say they're sorry, and I always think: What for? What they mean to say – what they should say – is that they're sorry to **hear** it.

"In training, in medical school, we're told to say we're sorry for someone's loss, when the worst happens, but even that's not adequate. I mean, if you say it all the time it sounds so hollow, so pointless… what can you say to someone who's just watched their loved ones die, often in agony and despair? How can you even begin to understand that unless you've been through it yourself? What words will ever bring comfort?"

He stopped, and I saw there were tears in his eyes. I reached over the table and put my hand on his, which was still fiddling with his knife.

"I understand," I said. "I've lost someone too." There was a catch in my voice, and I was close to tears myself.

He looked at me again. "I know," he said gently. "I know."

The food arrived before we could go on, and we both sighed and started to eat. The conversation was a little restrained after that. Neither Will nor I could really talk in detail about work, because of client confidentiality, so we chatted about what sort of music and films we liked, and what we'd seen on television lately – trivial subjects.

I wanted to ask him about his wife, but didn't feel able. As far as I was concerned I'd already ruined the evening.

To make matters worse, neither of us wanted dessert, which may have given us time to recover and relax – I was too full, because I hadn't been eating much lately, and Will claimed he was watching his waistline, although it looked slim enough to me. I suspected he just wanted the night to end.

I finished my wine and refused another one, while Will kept sipping his water and making me feel like an alcoholic.

"Coffee?" he said after a while. I shook my head. "No thanks – it gives me a headache if I drink it after a meal." Oh for goodness' sake, this was getting beyond a joke.

Will insisted on paying the bill, which made me a little annoyed, because I like to share, but he wouldn't take any money from me, and then we walked to his car.

He drove me home almost in silence, kissed my cheek on the doorstep, and left without saying goodbye. I was in bed, crying, by 10.

Chapter 20

The date had been so bad I really didn't expect to hear from Will ever again, but the next morning, while vacuuming the house, I received a text: Sorry. My fault. Can we just pretend it never happened and start again? x

I replied straight away: Pretend what happened? X

Will sent back: I'm free Tues. Fancy the pub this time? I'll have smthing that looks alcoholic. :)

I told him I did, and got on with my housework with renewed vigour.

....

The next day, Sunday, was my mother's 70th birthday, and I had to do the daughterly duty thing and go to her birthday meal, which was being held at a pub close to her house a few miles away from mine.

I was dreading it, not because I disliked my mum – I loved her, of course, although she frequently drove me mad – but because there would be people there I had been actively avoiding for months, not least my sister.

Andrea had organised the whole thing, naturally – she loves to take charge – so I knew very little about who was going, or what she had planned, if anything. Knowing Andrea she'd probably paid for a Gospel choir to sing Happy Birthday or bought a cake in the shape of an angel. So far she'd told me the place and time, and that was it.

I had to get a taxi to the venue, as there were no buses on a Sunday and it was too far to walk. I arrived ten minutes before the allotted time, bearing a card and gift – a bottle of expensive perfume, as mum loved scent – and went in, looking around for anyone I recognised.

Suddenly I heard Andrea's voice from across the room: "Steph! Where have you **been**? We've been waiting **ages** for you!"

I turned to see Andrea, immaculate as usual in a green, expensive-looking flowery dress and sensible black shoes, her hair up in a tidy bun on top of her head. She looked like an old-fashioned school mistress. She was hurrying towards me, one hand full of envelopes – cards, I supposed.

I was confused. "You told me two o'clock. It's ten to," I said.

Andrea looked at her watch – gold, of course – and tutted. "I said the **meal** was two o'clock," she scolded. "We're all sitting waiting. But don't worry, we've ordered for you. Come on." And she strutted off towards the back of the pub. I followed her reluctantly. Great start, I thought.

Andrea led me to a small function room at the rear of the restaurant. As we entered ten pairs of eyes turned to look at us, and I felt myself blushing.

Mum was sat at the head of the table like a queen, in front of her an assortment of people, most of whom I recognised. There was my Uncle John (mum's older brother), his wife, Aunt Sarah, and their middle-aged son Gary, who I'd never really liked. Sitting opposite them were mum's closest friend Alice, who I was sure was suffering from dementia these days, and Alice's husband, also John, who was a jolly man whose company I had long enjoyed.

There were balloons all along the table – silver ones with 70 printed on them. They were waving gently in the breeze from a slightly open window a few feet away. Despite the chill outside, it was quite warm in there.

I wanted to sit next to someone I liked, but Andrea ushered me to the end of the table furthest away from mum, where she'd left a place for me next to her and opposite her husband Tim, who I despised. So this was going to be a fun afternoon then, I thought.

I waved at mum, who was deep in conversation with a man next to her I didn't recognise, and she smiled at me before continuing to chat. I had already telephoned her that morning to say Happy Birthday, so I supposed it wasn't that rude to not say it now, although it felt like it.

"You sit here," Andrea said, and I obeyed, putting my coat on the back of the last chair at the table. I'd long been bossed around by my only sibling – as I think I've told you, she's three years older than me – and found it hard to break away from submissive habits formed over 39 years.

My sister went on: "I ordered you stuffed mushroom for starters and chicken for mains. That's OK isn't it? I know you like chicken, and we just couldn't wait any longer..." I was annoyed, but powerless, and feeling rather depressed, if truth be told, so said nothing. I didn't even like stuffed mushrooms.

As soon as I sat down I was aware of a jumble of noise coming from everyone on the table. As well as their voices, of course, I could hear their thoughts, tumbling over their speech, sometimes mimicking the sounds which issued from their mouths, at other times clashing with them.

I had got quite adept at ignoring people's thoughts over the last few months, but I was tired and unsettled, and knew I was going to find this event more than troubling. I tried to block the noise out, rubbed my forehead, then reached for the bottle of wine which stood in the middle of the table, and filled my glass. Maybe alcohol would help.

Oh dear, there she goes again.

I heard the thought issuing from Andrea at the exact same time she said the words: "Do you think that's wise, dear?"

"Yes, I do," I said, throwing her a hard stare as I sipped the wine. It was tepid and sweet, and rather horrible, if truth be told. *A bit like Andrea*, my inner voice added, and I nearly laughed.

She pursed her lips like a five-year-old. "Well, don't drink too much," she replied, moving the bottle back a bit further away than it had been. I rolled my eyes.

"So," she resumed, "how have you been? Work keeping you busy?"

"So-so," I said. I wasn't really in the mood to talk, and certainly not with her.

She tutted, and called over to Tim, who was talking to the man next to him. I didn't recognise him, and to be frank didn't care who he was. "Tim, dear," Andrea said, interrupting them, "tell Steph about your latest promotion."

Tim broke off his conversation and looked at his wife. He seemed a little irritated. "Oh, you tell her, darling, I was just chatting with Gordon here about church business. He's very interested in our latest campaign." And he turned back to Gordon, who looked horrified, to be honest. I immediately felt sorry for him.

Andrea patted my arm, and I almost flinched. "Tim's been appointed Head at St Bede's," she enthused. I must've been looking at her blankly, for she went on: "You know, St Bede's Grammar, in Castleton. It's the biggest secondary school in the town. A **grammar** school. Very strict. He doesn't start til the new year, but he's already had some very complimentary comments from the parents." I bet he has, I thought.

For want of anything productive to say, I muttered an "oh," and took a bigger gulp of my wine.

That was the beginning of an utterly awful afternoon. Because I wasn't speaking much Andrea spoke for both of us, yabbering constantly on about things I had absolutely no interest in. I responded with the odd 'mmm' or 'yeah,' but apart from that didn't get a word in edgeways. Tim kept giving me dark glances from his seat opposite, and at one point I was certain I heard him thinking *That girl is a bad influence.*

Yeah, right – one day I'd show him, I thought. Show him what I had no idea – by the time the mains came I was, to be honest, already a little tipsy.

The stuffed mushrooms had been hideous, so I left them largely untouched. The chicken was OK, if a little overcooked, but I ate most of it, washed down with more wine. Every time I filled my glass up Andrea tutted loudly – I didn't need to read her thoughts to know she disapproved.

After the plates had been cleared away, Andrea left the table, and I got a chance to speak to someone else. Sitting next to her – and before now largely hidden from view – was an elderly lady I recognised but couldn't place. I vaguely remembered her being at Harry's funeral, although most of that had been a blur, thankfully.

I squinted at her through my alcoholic haze, and smiled what I hoped was a winning smile. She smiled back, and pushed her glasses up on her nose.

"Stephanie, my dear, how delightful to see you again," she said.

I nodded, unsure what to respond when I didn't even know who she was. "Er... you too... er..."

The lady smiled again. "I'm Ada," she said. "I used to be your mum's neighbour when she was in Adelaide Street – you remember?"

I did, and said so. "Of course, Ada... how are you these days? Are you still there?" I was painfully aware my voice was a little slurred.

The woman shook her head. "Oh no, I'm in sheltered accommodation now – best thing I ever did. Since David died – he was my husband, you remember? – I was fed up of rattling around in that big old house, with all that cleaning to do. It's fantastic – they have a warden to look after you, and communal areas if you fancy a chat. We have bingo on Saturdays."

I hate it there.

Her unspoken thought came as clear as if she'd said it out loud, and for a moment it threw me, and I sat there not knowing what to say. I blinked at her. She was still smiling.

Then Andrea came back, and sat between us, blocking my view again. I was almost thankful.

Chapter 21

Andrea insisted we all have dessert, although I really didn't want any, and just picked at my sticky toffee pudding and custard until I felt sick and had to stop.

"We all have to have three courses, so we can split the bill easier," she had announced to the table in general, after a few people had mumbled dissent faced with a course they didn't want. But there was no going against Andrea when she was in full school ma'am mode, and mum, too, insisted, so Andrea got her way. There were more than a couple of half-eaten desserts to join my own, I was pleased to see, when the waiter cleared them away.

"And now for the cake!" shouted Andrea above the general hubbub, as the last plate and used napkin vanished into the kitchen.

There was an audible groan, and Andrea looked annoyed. "Oh, we don't have to eat it now," she said, "you can all take a piece home with you. I brought some bags."

In fact we had to wait another five minutes before the cake was brought in, candles ablaze, by a waiter and waitress half-heartedly singing Happy Birthday. Everyone joined in, like you have to, Andrea and I singing "Happy birthday dear mum" while most people sang "Dot" and a few "Dorothy." Mum, looking suitably embarrassed, managed to spit all over the cake while blowing out her candles – I made a mental note not to eat any – and everyone cheered and clapped.

I suddenly needed another drink, but there wasn't any wine left. Andrea had stopped me ordering another bottle once the one nearest me had gone, and the other two on the table had also been drained, I saw.

I decided to take matters into my own hands, and got up to go to the bar. "Where are you going?" demanded my sister. "We haven't finished yet. We're going to have coffee next."

"Fuck the coffee, I'm going for a drink," was what I meant to say, but instead it somehow came out as an irritable "I'm just going to the bog. Is that OK?" My sister winced; I knew she always called it the lavatory, and hated my crude, childish word for it. Probably why I used it.

I did in fact go to the toilet – I was actually bursting from all the wine I had drunk – but on the way back I bought a brandy from the bar, which I downed almost in one straight away, standing up. I didn't want Andrea to see me drinking – she'd only nag at me.

Feeling a little lightheaded, as well as hugely bloated from all the food, I resisted the temptation to just head for home (after all, my coat was still on my chair) and went back into the over-warm function room. I had difficulty walking in a straight line, but managed it without banging into a wall.

Instead of going back to my chair, I headed to see mum at the other end of the table, ignoring the hard stare from Andrea as I passed her. Mum was talking to my Aunt Sarah, but when I stood by her she turned to me. "Stephanie," she trilled. "How nice of you to come."

"I'm your daughter, I had to," I half-joked. She laughed a little too loudly for it to be genuine.

"Happy birthday, mum," I said then, bending down to kiss her on the cheek. "You having a nice one?"

Mum waved in the general direction of the table full of people, and said: "Of course. Look at all these lovely people who've come to help me celebrate. How could I not enjoy their company?" Well I certainly wasn't, but I didn't say anything. Unlike me, mum had always enjoyed being the centre of attention.

"Well, I'll be off now, mum," I said, then, remembering, "did Andrea give you my present?" Andrea had taken my gift and card from me as soon as she accosted me on the way in.

Mum looked blank. "Oh, I haven't done the presents yet, dear. But I'm sure it's lovely, whatever it is." Yeah, sure. I wouldn't be surprised if Andrea just threw it in the bin.

"Oh well, I'll be off now," I repeated, really wanting to get out of there as soon as was humanly possible. Preferably to go home and drink myself into oblivion. It felt like one of those nights.

Mum grabbed my arm with her old woman's hand. "No, no, you can't go just yet," she said. "Andrea has ordered coffee, and you must wait for a piece of my cake. Have you seen how beautiful it is?" And with her free hand she pointed at the cake sitting on the table in front of her. Aunt Sarah was carefully cutting it into pieces with a cake knife presumably provided by the venue, but I could see it was pink and yellow, flowery and had the words 'Happy 70th Mum' scrawled across it in icing. Well, it now said 'appy 70th Mu,' but I got the drift.

"Yes, it's... lovely," I mumbled. *Hideous*, I thought, and had to stifle a guffaw. *Thank goodness other people can't hear my thoughts like I can hear theirs.*

Mum gave me a sideways glance, and as I pulled my arm away from her clutch, for the first time in ages I consciously focussed in on someone's thoughts.

She's clearly drunk. And at my birthday do, too. Why can't she be more like Andrea? Mum was thinking.

I was so taken aback I almost staggered under the weight of it – or was that the alcohol? I'm not sure. Either way, I had to put both hands on the table to steady myself, and my stomach lurched. Aunt Sarah stopped cake-cutting and looked at me, obviously concerned. "Are you alright, Steph?" she asked. "You've gone a bit pale."

I muttered something even I didn't catch, and stared at mum. *Go on*, I thought at her, *think something else I can hate you for.*

She didn't disappoint.

Her voice, suddenly cold, said: "I think you've had a touch too much to drink, dear. Maybe you should go home after all," but her thoughts, clear as day despite my inner alcoholic turmoil, were much more venomous: *It's just as well Harry is gone. You'd have been a terrible example. Maybe God took him because He knew what would happen if He left him with you.*

My face drained of blood, my stomach gave another lurch and I turned to face my mother.

"How dare you?" I spluttered loudly, forgetting that she didn't know I could hear her inner thoughts. I was aware everyone on the table was watching now, silent and serious, but I didn't care. As far as I was concerned this was between me and mum.

"How **dare** you?" I repeated, even louder. Mum looked shocked, and recoiled a little, and suddenly I felt restraining arms around my shoulders. I turned to see Tim, with Andrea behind him. I swear she was smiling. Her husband was trying to drag me away, but I shrugged him off. "Get your fucking Bible-bashing hands off me, you ignorant, bigoted, hypocritical bastard," I spat. I heard Andrea squeak with fright, and Tim stepped away from me as if I would somehow contaminate him.

I turned back to mum, uncaring now that I was spoiling her birthday party. I certainly had drunk too much, and by now the alcohol was beginning to react with the unusually large amount of food I had eaten in a short space of time. It was also really warm in there, which wasn't helping. My stomach was growling and lurching in an alarming manner, and I knew I should leave, but I couldn't stop myself.

"You've always loved Andrea more than me – you made that very clear from the moment I was born," I said, quietly now. There was a gasp from someone at the table, but I didn't look to see who it was.

Mum's face had gone hard and cold, and she tried to say something, but I spoke over her: "But I don't expect you to be glad that Harry is no longer here. I know you loved him," I was crying now, and my stomach was making gurgling noises, "but no-one loved him more than me. And I was a good mother, d'you hear? A very good fucking mother. Unlike you!"

And then, as if to put a decisive end to a catastrophically terrible afternoon, I lurched forward and threw up all over the table, the cake and my mother; not once but twice, the second time spraying Aunt Sarah and the floor in equal measure.

All I remember next is being hurried out of the room and thrown into a taxi, alcohol-scented vomit still clinging to my clothes and dripping onto the cab floor. The driver made me pay extra "for the clean-up."

Chapter 22

I woke up next morning with the mother of all hangovers and little recollection of the previous day. My head felt like it was about to explode, my stomach felt empty and full at the same time and my arms and legs ached.

When my alarm went off at seven I turned it off and went back to sleep. Nearly two hours later I woke again, looked at the clock on my bedside table through blurry eyes and my heart nearly stopped. It was eight minutes to nine, and I was due in work at nine.

"Shit." I clambered out of bed, every nerve complaining, and staggered to the bathroom, where I dry-heaved into the sink for a few minutes. My clothes from the day before were still in the bath, where I'd obviously thrown them. They were covered in vomit. I could see bits of what looked like half-digested sticky toffee pudding. I decided to ignore them until I felt more human.

There was no way I was going to be able to make it to work, let alone sit through several hours of advising others, so I went back to the bedroom, grabbed my phone and rang Gary, my boss.

He answered on the second ring. "Hi Steph," said his cheery voice. Hearing him made me feel guilty, but there was nothing I could do about it. "I take it you're not coming in today?"

I croaked something about being ill, and sorry, and that I'd let him know later how I felt, and he rang off. Luckily I knew I only had a couple of appointments planned that day, so he'd be able to cover.

Then I went back to bed, pulled the covers over my head and tried to sleep. My mind kept attempting to take me back to the previous afternoon's events, but I refused to let it.

I was woken up some time later by my mobile's text alert noise. It seemed to be going every few minutes. At first I ignored it, but after a while it started annoying me and I reached for my phone and stuffed it under the pillows.

This only muffled the sound a little, however, and I could feel the phone's vibrations every time it went off, so a few minutes later I conceded defeat and sat up, grabbed the phone and, after rubbing the sleep out of my eyes, read the messages.

There were four texts from mum and six – six! – from Andrea. Groaning, I scrolled through them.

Mum: Thanks for ruining my party.

Andrea: Mum is rly upset. You shd b ashamed of urself.

Andrea: Every1 says u need help. I think u need a kick up the backside.

Mum: I will never forgive you.

Andrea: U o me £150. I'll be round later to collect it.

Andrea: That's 60 for the cake, 25 for meal and rest for cleaning bulls. (I presumed she meant bills, but was too upset to laugh).

Andrea: Bills.

Andrea: I'll come round this eve for the money.

And then there were two more from mum, which nearly broke my heart.

Mum: You're not my daughter anymore.

Mum: I don't want to see you again.

I was about to turn the phone off – I didn't want to get any more messages just now – when the alert went off again. It was Andrea. I'll pray for u, it said.

"Fuck off," I spat, and turned it off.

....

It was late afternoon before I got myself together. I put rubber gloves on to remove the wet and vomity clothes from the bath, rinsed the worst of the sick off with the shower, put them in the washing machine, had a shower myself, put some clean clothes on and made myself a cup of tea and a piece of toast.

My head was still hurting, so I swallowed two Paracetamol and went to sit on the sofa. As soon as I sat down Jess came in and meowed at me for food, so I had to get up again and feed him.

I turned the TV on and channel-flicked until I found something suitably undemanding to watch. I didn't want to think about what I had done the day before, but after a while my mind started replaying the afternoon's events like a truly bad film.

Did I really throw up on my mum's 70th birthday cake? In front of all her family and friends? I had to admit I could hardly believe it, but the evidence was irrefutable.

And then there was what I'd told her. I couldn't remember exactly what I said, but I knew it had been hateful, and very unwise. What would they think of me? Because of course they didn't know I was responding to mum's thoughts (even these I couldn't properly recall – though I knew it was something about Harry) – they probably thought I was deranged.

No… no, they knew I'd had a lot to drink. They must've just assumed I was drunk.

That was fine, let them. After all, I **had** been drunk. I'd had around half a bottle of wine and a brandy. Oh, and another glass of wine before I left the house. That was far more than I normally drank in one sitting.

Oh fuck, I thought, they'd never let me forget it, would they?

It was around six o'clock that Andrea turned up. I'd been expecting her, and although it was tempting to leave her on the doorstep in the rain, I opened the door and let her in.

She stood in the hallway, and I handed her an envelope with £150 cash in which I had earlier put by the door. I felt guilty for ruining mum's party, and didn't begrudge the money, although I did wonder how that hideous cake cost £60. Never mind, I'd let it pass.

She didn't say thank you, just glared at me. She had bags under her eyes and her hair was a bit messier than normal. Presumably she'd had a bad night too.

"Well?" I said. "Aren't you going to give me a lecture? Believe me, you can't make me feel any worse than I do already."

She pursed her lips in that irritating way she had. "You don't deserve us, you know," she said. This, to be frank, was the last thing I expected her to say.

I blinked at her. "Eh?" I said.

She leant against the wall, twiddling the envelope in her hands. I could smell her perfume, sweet and cloying, and my stomach turned over.

"You've always been a rebel, Steph," she said. "Always fancied yourself as better than us, but really you've been a disappointment all of your life."

I started to object, but she spoke over me, her voice calm and measured. I expected she'd been rehearsing this little speech all day.

"Skiving off school, smoking, drinking, going off with boys when you were just a child…"

"Now hang on," I interjected, but she was continuing: "Marrying that loser, and then not sticking to your marriage vows. It's no wonder he divorced you. And of course little Harry wouldn't have died if you'd…"

"Get out!" I shouted, angry as hell, stopping her mid-sentence.

How dare she say those things? How dare she criticise me? Just because I didn't share her pious beliefs about how to behave. And anyway, I only bunked off twice, smoked for six months until I came to my senses, and had my first boyfriend at 16 – old enough. I wasn't exactly a problem child. I never tried drugs or shoplifted, like so many of my schoolfriends, and only got drunk once or twice. Standard behaviour for a teenager.

She stared at me, unmoving, as cold as mum had been the day before. I opened the door again, and gestured for her to leave.

"Get out before I throw you out," I said between clenched teeth, and she could tell I meant it. She left without saying another word. I purposely blocked out her thoughts as she passed me – I could do without knowing what **they** were.

I slammed the door shut behind her, slumped to the hall floor and sobbed.

For, whatever else she said about me, however unjustified most of it was, I knew one thing had been true. It was **my** fault Harry died. **My** fault, and no-one else's.

Chapter 23

Later that evening I turned my phone back on – much as I wanted to shun the outside world, I couldn't avoid it forever.

There were no more texts from mum or Andrea, thank goodness, but there was one from Will, sent a couple of hours before, asking if I was still OK to go for a drink the following evening, Tuesday. Shit, I'd forgotten about that. I wasn't really in the mood to go for another date just yet, especially after the first disastrous one, and at that moment felt sure I'd never drink alcohol ever again, so I sent him a text: Sorry, smthing's come up. Maybe nxt wk?

He replied a few minutes later: You OK?

I smiled thinly as I typed in the reply: Fine. X

I added a kiss to show him I was still interested. A moment later, as I still had my mobile in my hand, it rang. It was Will.

"You're not going to get rid of me that easily," he said after I uttered a wary "Hello?"

"I don't know what you mean," I said, my voice a bit unsteady.

"I've been with enough women to know that when they say they're fine it usually means just the opposite," he said. He sounded kind, and gentle, and, as much as I tried to stop myself, I started to cry again.

"Steph?" he said. I could only blub down the phone at him. "Steph? Are you crying? Stay there, I'm coming round." And before I could protest, he rang off.

He arrived about 20 minutes later. I opened the door with a tissue in my hand, eyes red and nose blocked. I had hurriedly brushed my hair, but knew I was not a pretty sight. Still, I could hardly send him away again when he'd driven all this way.

As he came in he handed me a huge block of chocolate. "I thought this might make it better," he said, and I smiled through my dried tears. "How did you know?" I asked. He shrugged. "Lucky guess."

I ushered him into the living room and asked if he wanted a cup of tea. "Please," he said, then shouted "milk, no sugar" as I left him to go into the kitchen. Of course, he was sweet enough, I thought.

Five minutes later we were sitting on the sofa sipping hot tea and staring at the cat, who was plonked down in the middle of the floor washing himself noisily. "What's his name?" asked Will. "Jess," I said, and the cat looked over, tongue out mid-wash. "Sorry, her," said Will, and I laughed. "No, he's a he," I said. Will looked puzzled. "After Postman Pat's cat," I explained.

Jess abandoned his washing routine and strolled over to Will, who put his hand out invitingly. Jess nuzzled his fuzzy ginger face against Will's knuckles, and the doctor proceeded to stroke his furry head. "I thought Jess was black and white, as in 'Postman Pat and his black and white cat'," said Will, singing the refrain from the TV theme tune.

"He is. Our Jess isn't," I said. "Harry named him."

"Of course," said Will, continuing to stroke the now clearly very happy cat. "He looks like a Jess, don't you puss?"

"I take it you like cats," I said then, thinking about how little success he seemed to be having with his mother's hound of a dog.

Will looked at me and smiled. "Yeah. I used to have one. I love how honest they are – if they don't like you, you certainly know about it."

"Well I think he likes **you**," I said. "He just looks on me as someone who gives him food and the odd bit of warmth. I sometimes feel like his slave."

Will laughed, and picked his tea up from the coffee table. As he did, Jess jumped up onto his lap and settled himself down for his seventh nap of the day. "See," I said, "he likes you."

Will chuckled, and stroked the cat's head with his free hand.

"So," he said after a minute or two.

"So what?" I asked innocently, knowing full well what was coming.

"So, are you going to tell me what's been going on? I can tell you're very upset – I'm astute like that. Was it something I said?" I started to speak, but he went on: "I know our first date didn't go very well – we both made a bit of a mess of it, I think – but I thought we'd decided to give it a second chance. I thought you were looking forward to it."

"I was… I **am**," I said. "It's not you, it's something that happened yesterday, at my mother's 70th birthday party." I sniffed, trying to stop myself from crying again.

"Oh," said Will. "Go on… that's if you want to talk about it, that is."

I sighed heavily. "Suffice to say I… got a bit tipsy, had strong, rather cruel words with my mother and then threw up all over her cake."

Will stifled a laugh. "It's not funny, is it?" he asked.

"No, it's not," I said. "My mother's now disowned me, my sister hates me even more than she used to, if that's possible, and I have brought disgrace and humiliation to my entire family… not for the first time, if Andrea's to be believed."

Will mused over this for a minute, before saying: "You don't get on well with your sister then?"

Now it was my turn to laugh. "You must be joking," I said. "She's always hated me. I think she resented my arrival – she was three when I was born, and spoilt rotten by all accounts. Even when we were kids she used to take my toys away from me when I displeased her, which seemed to be every day. And when we were older she disapproved of every decision I made."

"A clash of personalities?" asked Will, putting his half-empty cup down on the table, causing Jess to give him an indignant 'how dare you move' look.

I thought for a second. "I suppose you could say that," I said. "She's an evangelical Christian, for starters, while I…"

"You're not going to tell me you don't believe in our Lord and Saviour Jesus Christ, are you?" interrupted Will, sounding shocked.

I stared at him, unsure whether he was joking. Just as my heart was beginning to sink, he gave it away by laughing out loud. "Ha!" he said. "Your face!"

I reached across and hit him on the shoulder. "You bastard," I said, relieved. "I thought you were serious for a minute."

He was shaking his head, still laughing. "Sorry," he said, "I couldn't resist it. No, I'm a heathen, full-time confirmed atheist."

"Me too, thank God," I said, and we both laughed at the irony.

"So she disapproves of your lifestyle?" Will said then, turning serious again. "I mean, you're hardly a Satanist, are you? Unless you're not telling me something."

I shook my head. "I think she just hates the fact I don't believe in the same thing she does," I said. "Why it should mean so much to her I don't know – I mean, I don't hate **her** because she loves an imaginary being…"

"Don't you?" asked Will.

"No, I don't," I said. "She can worship what the hell she likes. I hate her because she's a hypocrite, preaching love thy neighbour at the same time as telling me I'm a bad person because I don't feel the same way as her. Telling me I'm immoral because I don't follow her ideas on what's right. I have morals – I know right from wrong. You don't have to believe in a higher power to believe being good is the right thing to be."

"Hear hear," said Will.

We sat in silence for a moment, and then I reached for the chocolate, opened it and broke a couple of pieces off, before offering the rest of the bar to the doctor. "Want some?" I asked. He shook his head. "I don't like it much," he said. "Too rich."

I dropped my jaw in mock surprise. "You.. don't… like… chocolate?" I whispered. "Get out of my house now, you weirdo." He laughed. "All the more for you," he said. "Oh yeah," I said, and put the two pieces in my mouth at the same time. They were rich and creamy, and delicious.

"So," continued my guest, "does your mother share your sister's religious beliefs?"

I shrugged, and swallowed the chocolate before answering. "Well, she certainly believes – it was she, not my dad, who instilled religion in Andrea; but she's more relaxed and less fervent, if that's the right word."

"Your dad still alive?" asked Will.

I shook my head sadly. "No, he died when I was 18. Lung cancer – he was a chain-smoker."

"Ah," said the doctor. "Mine too – and my mum. They died within a year of each other. Mum had bowel cancer, dad had a cardiac arrest ten months later. I was… 26 when I became an orphan.

Thankfully they both lived long enough to see me achieve my dream and become a GP."

"Any siblings?" I asked next. Will shook his head. "Only child," he replied.

"Lucky you," I said, smiling.

"Well, it certainly meant I got a better class of Christmas present," said the doctor.

Just then my text alert went off, and I retrieved my phone from the table to read it. "I expect it's Andrea telling me I'm damned or something," I said, laughing, but when I read it my heart sank.

"What's up?" asked Will, looking with concern at my serious face. I handed him the phone so he could read the message. It was from Gary, my boss, and said: Hope you're feeling better, but think it's best u take tomorrow off too. I heard about the party. Come in Wed and we can talk. X

Chapter 24

"Shit, shit, shit, shit, shit," I cursed, on the verge of tears again. Will handed me back the phone.

"Who's Gary?" he asked, sounding worried.

"My boss," I replied. "How the hell did he find out about yesterday?" Will looked confused, so I explained that I had taken today off sick because of my monumental hangover this morning, but that I had been planning to go back in tomorrow.

"Maybe your mum or sister told him?" suggested Will, but I shook my head. "No, I don't think even Andrea would stoop so low – she'd want to keep the incident as quiet as possible. No, it must've been someone else there."

"Shit," I went on. "He couldn't sack me, could he? Not for something I did out of work?" I was really concerned now. I didn't love my job by any means, but I didn't want to lose it.

Will patted me on the arm. "If he does you could take him to an industrial tribunal," he said, trying to be reassuring. It didn't work.

I picked my phone up again, and reread the message. "What the hell am I supposed to reply to that?"

Will shrugged. "Just say you're feeling better, but will take tomorrow off to make sure, and will be happy to talk on Wednesday," he offered.

"Should I ring him?" I asked. "Maybe I should talk about it today? Get it over with?"

Will shook his head. "No, whatever he wants to talk about can wait until you're feeling less emotional. A day off will do you good – and maybe give him time to think, too. Don't worry about it, Steph, it'll be fine, I'm sure. Is he a good boss?"

"Usually," I said. "He's really nice."

"In that case I'm sure he won't be too concerned about one out-of-hours drunken incident," said Will, resuming stroking Jess, who was still on his lap. "And anyway, he's done you a favour."

I looked sideways at him. "What do you mean?" I asked.

"Well, I'm off tomorrow, too, as you know. How d'you fancy a walk in the countryside followed by lunch at a riverside pub instead of slaving away at the office? With me, I mean." He looked sheepish, and I had to laugh.

"That'd be lovely," I said, and meant it.

Will left an hour or so later, as I was tired and needed some sleep. On the way out he kissed me on the lips – a lovely, soft, gentle kiss which left me wanting more.

………………………………………………..

The next day dawned cold but bright, one of those pleasant autumn days when you can appreciate the season.

Will picked me up at 10 on the dot, and we drove about 12 miles out of town to a pretty bit of national parkland which I used to frequent when Gerry and I were together. I hadn't been there for years, but remembered it fondly.

We left the car in the car park and strolled through the countryside, kicking up leaves and breathing in the fresh autumn air. As we went we talked about everything from our favourite season to what type of films we enjoyed. It was nice, and I forgot about everything else for a while.

After a couple of miles we came to a lake, and sat down on a bench to watch the birds.

"I used to come here with Mia," said Will suddenly, and my heart sank a little.

"Me and Gerry came here too," I said sadly. I found it sad to talk about our previous partners – and a little inappropriate, to be honest.

Will was silent, and I realised I didn't even know how his wife had died. I was just wondering whether – and how – I should ask, when Will told me. I had a feeling this is why he'd brought me here.

"She had breast cancer," he started. "Found a lump in one breast, which turned out to be malignant, so she had a mastectomy. Then they found it had spread to the other breast, so she had that off, too."

"That must've been hard," I said.

"It was terrible," he said. "But then she found out she was pregnant."

I gasped, and he gave me a sideways look. "Yeah, that was even worse," he said quietly.

"So she…" I didn't know how to go on.

"She refused to have any other treatment, because of the baby," continued Will. "No chemo, no radiotherapy, no nothing…"

"I can understand that," I said, and I did. As a mother, I knew you'd do anything – anything – to protect your child.

"Well, I tried to persuade her otherwise, being a doctor an' all, I knew what was likely to happen if she didn't have treatment. And I was right."

"It got worse?" I offered, knowing of course that the ending to this story was not a happy one.

He nodded and sighed. "The cancer spread, and by the time we realised it, it was too late for her… and the baby. She was 22 weeks' pregnant when she died. When they died."

I put my hand on Will's arm. "I'm sor… I mean, that must have been traumatic for you."

"It was," Will said simply. "It took me around two years to start to feel myself again. Before I realised life really **was** worth living, despite the tragedies which many people face."

He went silent, and we sat and watched the ducks paddling on the lake. There was no-one else around.

"Was it a boy or a girl?" I asked. It seemed to be an important question.

Will smiled sadly. "A little girl," he said. "We called her Amelia."

"Beautiful," I said. "Yes," said Will. "She was."

We sat for a while in silence. A couple of dog-walkers strolled past, followed by two young women holding hands and a man pushing a toddler in a buggy. Something startled the ducks, and a few of them flapped off into the bushes at the side of the lake. It reminded me of the last time I had been near water.

"That boy," I said suddenly, "the one in the lake. Do you know how he is now?"

"He's fine," said Will. "I asked about him at the weekend, and they said he was doing great. He's still in hospital but should be discharged soon."

A weight seemed to have been lifted from my shoulders, and I said: "Good. That's good. It was lucky you were there to save him."

Will stood up and turned to look at me. "I'm a doctor, it's what I do," he said. "Sometimes, I save people. Not everyone, not all the time, but sometimes. And that makes it all worthwhile."

We walked back to the car almost in silence, me contemplating sadness and how much of it many of us have to endure during our short lives.

Will drove us a bit further away from town to a riverside pub he knew, where we had a light lunch and a pot of tea in the beer garden overlooking the river. It was chilly, but we kept our coats on so we could enjoy the view.

We talked about more pleasant subjects, and ended up laughing hysterically at a funny story Will told about one of his patients.

On the drive back I asked if he would drop me off at my mother's instead of taking me straight home.

"Is that wise?" he asked.

"Probably not," I said, "but I have to try to talk to her before Andrea gets to her – if she hasn't already."

So Will dropped me outside my mother's door – I knew she'd be in, because she had a strict weekly routine and was always home on a Tuesday afternoon – and drove off, waving, after promising to ring me later for an update.

I rang the doorbell and waited, feeling like a naughty pupil going to see the headmaster.

Chapter 25

Mum took some time getting to the door, as she wasn't as mobile as she used to be, so I had a minute or so to wait on the doorstep. My anxiety increased.

"Steph?" she said when at last she opened the door. She sounded pleased to see me, which I was surprised at, to be honest. Last time I saw her she was staring at me with anger in her eyes and my vomit on her dress.

"Can I come in?" I asked, and she opened the door wider so I could.

We went to sit in her kitchen – she lived in a small bungalow, and the kitchen was where she spent most of her time. It was a big room, but cosy and comfortable, with a small dining table and four chairs on one side for when she had visitors. She usually sat in a large armchair in the corner, next to a real fire – it was an old house – and she sat there now. The fire was blazing. I stayed standing up.

"What do you want, Steph?" she said, once she'd settled down in her chair like a queen on a golden throne. "I didn't expect to see you for some time, after Sunday's incident. Thought you'd be too ashamed to show your face, to be honest." She was efficient and to-the-point, as ever. Mum used to be a teacher before she retired, and sometimes you could still tell.

"I wanted to say sorry," I said, which was true. Whatever mum had said – or thought – I had no right upsetting her in a public place.

She shrugged. "I'd be amazed if you weren't sorry," she said. "I brought you up to respect people, didn't I?"

"Yes, you did," I said, because she seemed to be expecting a reply.

"What you did on Sunday was inexcusable. Everyone was shocked. I expect I'll never live it down. Everybody's talking about it."

"Really?" I asked. "Is that how my boss knows?"

She looked sharply at me, still standing. "Well I never told him, but I'm not surprised," she said. "It's a small town; there were a lot of people there."

"Yes," I said. "I suppose I deserve to face consequences for my behaviour." I was still feeling sorry for myself, if truth be told.

"Well, like all of us you'll have to face your Maker eventually, and answer for **all** your sins," she said, and I sighed. I really didn't want to get into a theological argument at this point, so said nothing.

"Sit down," she said then, motioning me to the nearest dining chair. I turned it round to face her, and obediently sat.

Mum was fiddling with her wedding ring nervously. "I'm sorry about the texts," she said, after a short pause. "About… not wanting to see you again, and… whatever else I said. I was very upset. I didn't really mean it."

I flapped my hand at her in that way you do when you want to dismiss what someone is saying. "It's OK," I said. "We all say things we don't mean sometimes."

"You said I was a bad mother," she said, quiet now.

I looked at her old, wrinkled face, her silver-grey hair still full and shoulder-length, her eyes still clear. She seemed sad. "Well, I didn't mean that, either," I said. "I'd drunk too much, and eaten too much, and wasn't very well. It was the alcohol talking."

"Yes, yes," she said, efficient again. "I did tell you. You should've gone home when I told you to, instead of ranting at me in a frankly deranged manner." I stared at her and stayed silent. This was a mistake, for she saw it as a sign I wanted her to continue with the lecture. "Andrea said you were drinking wine like it was going out of fashion, and I can believe it. I mean, my dress reeked of alcohol – I had to throw it in the bin, and it was a designer one, too."

She paused for breath, and I took the opportunity to say something. This was another mistake. "You said you were glad Harry died," I said quietly, staring at the fire, angry again. "How could you say such a thing?"

Mum gasped loudly, and I looked up at her. "I never said such a thing! Why would I?" She sounded puzzled.

And then it hit me. She hadn't actually said she was glad Harry was no longer with us – she'd thought it, instead. "I… I mean," I said.

"I adored Harry, and you know it. How could you suggest I'd be happy to see him dead?" she sounded genuinely bemused, which angered me more than ever, because I knew – I **knew** – she'd been thinking just that.

"You didn't say it, mum, but you were thinking it."

"What do you mean? Of course I…" she stopped mid-sentence, and her eyes widened. Presumably she was remembering exactly what had happened the moment before I vomited all over her party.

I know I should've stopped then. I should have confused her with some made-up explanation, but… I couldn't. Call it weakness, call it a desire to unburden myself, call it whatever the hell you like, but I felt I had to seize the moment and tell her – tell anyone, really – what I could do. I had to tell her my secret, while she'd believe me. So I did.

"I can read minds, mum."

She stared at me, then frowned.

"Ever since Harry died, I can read people's minds. Not just people's, either – animals and even some plants, too; I can hear what they're thinking… or feeling, in the case of animals."

"No… don't be ridiculous," she was saying, but I went on, calm and cool now: "I've learnt how to block them out, most of the time, but if I want to, or if I'm tired, or emotional, I can hear what people around me are thinking, as clear as I hear them speak."

She was shaking her head. "Don't be ridiculous, Steph," she repeated. "Nobody can read minds. It's just a trick. I don't know why you're saying this – do you think it'll stop me being upset about what you did?"

I stared at her. "Think something now," I said. "Go on, anything – make it something weird, so I couldn't possibly guess it. I guarantee you I will tell you what you're thinking."

She was still shaking her head, and laughing nervously. I tried to read her mind, but there was nothing there.

"**Please**," I said, desperate now. "Let me prove it to you. I'm not mad."

She looked me in the eyes, and I read her thoughts: *The Devil is in you, girl.*

I smiled. "It's not the Devil, mum – there's no such thing."

Mum looked surprised, frowned, and I heard another thought. It was clear: *The pink sausages David ate at the barbecue gave him salmonella.*

I repeated her thought back to her, word for word: "The pink sausages David ate at the barbecue gave him salmonella. I dunno who David is, but everyone knows you don't eat undercooked sausages." I smiled at her – I don't know why; I'd just scared the life out of her.

"It's a trick," she was saying, but I shook my head. "Think something else," I prompted, eager now to show off my new skill.

She stared at the fire, and I heard: *The chimney needs to be swept before winter comes.*

"The chimney needs to be swept before winter comes. I suppose you're right," I said cheerily.

Suddenly mum stood up from her chair, obviously flustered. Her face was white. I stood up too, but she brushed me aside and went to the door. I followed her, unsure where this was leading.

At the kitchen door she turned to face me. "I want you to leave now," she said slowly, as if to a child.

"But mum..." I started.

"Whatever you can do, you need to stop it now," she said, sounding upset and scared. She walked away, and I followed. "Things like that are not Godly. They're the Devil's work. Please leave." And she carried on to the front door and opened it. I stood in the hallway.

"There's no such thing as the Devil," I said. "This has nothing to do with evil. I'm not an evil person!" I almost yelled this last bit, and she winced. I could tell she was frightened.

She just held the door open, unspeaking. I decided it was pointless trying to reason with her – maybe I could come back in a few days and try again – so I left. As I passed her, I said: "Please don't tell anyone – don't tell Andrea." I sounded rather desperate; I was already regretting my actions.

She said nothing, and shut the door behind me as soon as I was through it.

Great, I thought. That was a resounding success, then.

When Will rang me that evening to see how I'd got on with mum, I just murmured that we'd both said we were sorry, which was true, but that we'd had words again, which was also true. I didn't elaborate on what we had words about, of course, and he didn't ask.

I went to bed feeling empty and depressed. I cried myself to sleep.

Chapter 26

The next day, Wednesday, I went back to work with a feeling of dread in my stomach. It wasn't just that I was regretting letting mum in on my secret, and worried she'd tell Andrea what I'd said, I was also terrified of what Gary was going to say to me about the weekend's events.

He couldn't sack me, could he?

As soon as I got to work, and sat down in my office to go through the post and emails, Gary knocked on my open door.

"Oh hi," I said, sounding far more cheerful than I felt. "Come in."

He entered the room, shutting the door behind him, and sat on one of the chairs clients usually used. I could hardly look him in the face, I was that ashamed.

His first words were encouraging, though. "Are you feeling better, Steph?" he asked. Gary was a kind and generous boss, and a good man, as far as I could work out. I had hopes he'd be understanding.

I closed my laptop so we could talk without any distractions. "Yes, fine," I said. Although this wasn't entirely true, I was certainly feeling better – physically, at least – than I had been on Monday.

"Good. Good," he said, and coughed in a nervous fashion. "I… er… it's a bit awkward, but I need to speak to you about what happened at your mum's party."

I put my hands together on the table, as if to close off any negative thoughts. My heart was racing. "How do you know what happened at my mother's party, if you don't mind me asking?"

"Well," he said, half laughing in that way you do when you're about to give bad news and don't know how to phrase it, "the pub manager is one of my best friends – Brian; you won't know him – and he had to clean up the, er, mess you left and sort out the guests after you'd gone home. I believe it was he who put you in a taxi."

"Oh." There seemed to be nothing else to say.

"He recognised you from a function we'd been to once – anyway, he knew you worked for me – and he felt it was necessary to tell me."

"Did he now."

"No, not in a negative way, Steph – honestly, he's a nice man, is Brian – but he was concerned about you. He said you were in a bad way, and he wanted to check you were alright afterwards. Honest."

I looked up at him – until then I had been staring at my hands – and smiled weakly. "Well, I'm fine," I said, gentler now. "You can tell him that."

"I don't believe you, Steph," he said then. "You keep forgetting you're still in mourning."

I started. "I never forget that, Gary, I can assure you," I said, a little riled.

He was shaking his head. "No, of course not, I just mean you have to go easy on yourself – and your family do, too."

"Maybe you should tell them," I said shortly.

He looked me in the eyes. "Maybe I should."

There was a pause, and then he added: "Anyway, I just wanted to remind you that if you need any time off – any time at all – just let me know. I can always cover – you know I don't do much client work these days, so I'm usually around. And if you ever want to talk, I'm here."

He sounded so kind, and understanding, that tears sprang to my eyes. "Th- thank you," I said.

He got up then, and went to leave. As he had his hand on the door, he turned back. "Oh, news about the McDonoughs," he said, sounding more business-like.

I sniffed away my tears. "What about them?" I asked.

"The council said they'll only fund two more sessions each, now they're being seen separately. So you only have two more weeks to bring them to any sort of conclusion."

"Oh fabulous," I said with heavy irony.

....

It so happens I saw Mrs McDonough – sorry, the former Mrs McDonough, now reverted to her maiden name of Susan Shaw – that Friday.

She was noticeably happier and more talkative when her brute of an ex-husband was not in the same room as her, and even looked brighter and more alive, somehow.

We started by catching up on her situation. She informed me she and the two children were now living in emergency accommodation, which was a bedsit on the edge of town, but that it wasn't too bad. The people who lived in the same house were generally quite nice, and she was close enough to the kids' school to be able to walk them there and back.

"And the council said they should be able to get us a permanent place before Christmas," she enthused, sounding quite excited by the prospect. I could've told her the council always promised that, and usually failed to deliver, but decided not to burst her bubble.

"That'll be good," I said. "How is Stuart doing? Do you see him at all?"

She shook her head. "I dunno where he is," she said. "The last I saw of him he was still in the old flat, just before they came to take everything away."

"Oh, right. Well, we have a mobile number for him, so I'll give him a ring and see if I can find out what's happening over him seeing the boys," I said. "Have you not tried ringing him?"

"No. I don't want him to see them," she said.

"Well, he is their father, and the court has said he can see them as long as he gives you notice, isn't that right?" I said, consulting the latest correspondence.

"Yeah, but they don't miss him."

"You don't really know that," I said, as gently as I could. "They'll say so just to please you – children that age don't know how to communicate properly, so they'll say what they think you want them to say. He's been there their whole lives, so they're bound to miss him being around. He wasn't a bad dad, was he?"

Susan looked away. "No…" she started.

"But?" I asked.

"No, no buts," she said, "he was a good father to the kids. Loving, kind, playful… pity he couldn't be like that with everyone else, too."

"Well, we'll be in touch with him anyway, because he has a couple of sessions with us before we finish seeing you both."

"I have a job!" she suddenly announced, and I almost clapped.

"Great," I said. "What?"

"It's only a cleaning job – pretty basic, really – but it suits me fine. It's at the Royal Hotel near the hospital – you know?" I nodded. "Part-time, just mornings, while the kids are in school. So I get to pick them up after. The pay's not bad."

"That's fabulous," I said. "It'll give you a bit more money to play with, and help your self-confidence, too. I bet the children notice a difference."

She looked puzzled. "I mean, that you're a happier mummy," I explained.

She smiled. "Yeah. Little Ewan told me I looked pretty the other day," she laughed.

"They're sweet at that age," I said, "You ought to cherish it." And for a moment Harry's chubby little face came back to me, and I almost howled in pain.

"Yeah."

We talked about a few other issues she had, but I was really pleased with her. It was nothing to do with my help, truth be told, but I felt like she'd started to turn her life around and would be able to give her boys a better start from now onwards.

As she put her coat on ready to leave, I reminded her that next week's session would be our last. She almost looked sad. "I was just beginning to enjoy them!" she said, and I laughed.

"Well, you don't really need me anymore," I said. "But have a think, and if there's anything you want to talk about next week, just let me know."

She smiled and left.

As soon as she had gone I picked up the phone and dialled the number I had for her ex-husband's mobile. He answered on the second ring.

"Hello?" He sounded drunk, and my heart sank.

"Mr McDonough?" I asked.

"Who's askin'?"

"It's Stephanie Martin from Dempsey Counsellors," I replied, trying to sound official. "I'm ringing to confirm the time of our next session."

"I don't wanna see you no more," he slurred.

"I'm sorry, Mr McDonough, but I've been informed that if you don't attend your sessions you may have your benefits stopped." This wasn't entirely true, but I really wanted to see him again, and felt the lie could only benefit him.

He swore, and I went on: "You only have two more to come to, and then we will leave you in peace. Your next session is booked for Monday at 11am. Can you assure me you'll be here?"

He grunted, which I took for a yes. I really wanted to talk to him again, if only to reassure myself he was not going to do anything silly, so I added: "It really will be beneficial to you to come along, Mr McDonough. We can talk about how your contact with the boys is going."

He mumbled something I didn't catch. "I'm sorry," I said, "I didn't get that – the reception's not very good."

"The bitch won't let me see them," he repeated, louder, and I sighed.

"Your ex-wife can't refuse you access unless there's a good reason," I said. "And she knows this. We can talk about it on Monday if you like, and sort it out properly for you."

"OK," he said. He actually sounded relieved.

"Good. See you then."

Little did I know it was to be a session I would remember all my life.

Chapter 27

I had a quiet weekend, just going for walks, reading the paper and watching crap TV. I felt like recharging my batteries was important, so didn't see anyone – I even turned Jenny down when she phoned to see if I wanted to go clothes shopping with her. Peace and quiet was what I craved, so I got some.

Of course everywhere I looked Harry was there. Not actually, of course – I may have been hearing things, but I wasn't seeing them too. But the echo of him always followed me everywhere I went.

At first I had found this intolerably sad, but as time went on it became comforting, in a way. I was coming to realise that although Harry was gone, he would always be a part of me – literally, because it was I who created him in the first place.

Monday dawned wet and cold, but I felt pretty positive. I had finally been in touch with Stuart McDonough's social worker the previous week – she had cancelled our arranged meetings twice, and I had given up trying to make another one.

Cathy Hancock was pretty uninformative, to be honest, and only told me a few things I didn't already know.

One of these was that Stuart was currently living at the house of a friend of a friend, but that this was very much a temporary arrangement – if council accommodation wasn't found for him in a couple of weeks' time (which seemed highly unlikely, given the fact he was now single, male, jobless **and** an ex-prisoner), he would be, as she put it, "having to find his own way." I took this to mean he would be homeless. She didn't sound all that worried. I supposed she had other, to her more important, clients to think about.

Stuart McDonough was ten minutes late for his appointment, and I was beginning to think he wasn't going to show, when he walked into my office without knocking.

He stumbled through the door as if he had the weight of the world on his shoulders, then shuffled across the carpet to the chair like a man twice his age. I could smell the alcohol even from three feet away.

He looked dirty, as if he hadn't washed for weeks. His hair was long and matted, and I wondered bleakly if he even had a brush to his name any more. He was wearing the same clothes I had seen him in last time we met. Again, no coat, despite the fact it was blowing a gale and throwing it down outside. His torn jeans and holey t-shirt were soaked through, and he was forming puddles on the floor by the chair legs.

To be honest I didn't know quite how to start the conversation, despite all my training.

"Glad you could make it," was the best I could do at short notice. I was immediately ashamed of myself for saying it, because it sounded like sarcasm, although it wasn't meant to be.

He grunted. "I didn't have much choice, did I?" he muttered. His voice was slurred again, and I idly wondered how much he had had to drink that day already.

"Well," I said, "I **am** glad to see you. I hear you're staying at a friend's house at the moment. How's that working out for you?"

He stared at the wall a few inches above my head. "It's shit," he mumbled.

"Oh? Why?"

"Well, the guy's letting me kip on his sofa, right, but he's out all day at work and most evenings, so I'm on me own a lot. Not that I want him around anyway, he's a fuckin' bore."

"He's a friend of a friend, yes?"

"Old mate of Andy's, yeah. Fuckin' Paki."

I blinked. "Excuse me?" I said, taken aback.

"He's a fuckin' Paki," he said, with some venom. "One of them bastard Muslims, for all I know. Always goin' on about my bad habits and naggin' me like he's me mum. I bet he's plannin' some terrorist thing with his mates down the pub every night. I can't even pronounce his name."

I was somewhat shocked by the casual racism, but decided now was not the time for a lecture. "Er... well, he's been good enough to put you up when no-one else would," I said, desperate to change the subject.

"He's only doin' it cos he owes Andy a favour," said Stuart. "And once the fortnight's up, he's kickin' me out. Told me so."

"Do you have anywhere else to go?" I asked.

Stuart looked me in the eyes, and his own were blank and bleak as the ocean. "Nowhere."

We talked a little bit more about how he could improve his immediate future – I gave him some leaflets on council initiatives which may help – but I knew he wasn't really listening. He seemed to have given up on life, and I was becoming increasingly worried the more I spoke to him.

I asked him if he'd seen his sons since the family had split up, and he snarled. "Not once," he said. "Every time I ring up the bitch won't even let me speak to them. She's not allowed to do that, is she?"

"Well," I said, "as Susan has full parental responsibility now she can more or less choose when and where you see them, but I'm sure she'll come round once you get yourself together again."

He stayed silent, so I added: "She knows you love them, and are a good dad when you're with them, and she also knows they need both of their parents. Stay in touch with her, and try to stay on good terms, and she'll let you see the boys soon, I'm sure."

"Yeah, well I don't think that's gonna happen this side of the apocalypse," he said, kicking the chair leg with the back of his right foot.

"Can't you do something, Miss?" he said then, almost pleading. I told him I was still seeing his ex-wife, and that I kept reminding her of the importance of children having access to both parents, so I had every hope that she would be reasonable very soon.

He didn't look convinced.

"Me own dad left when I was seven," he said then, even though I hadn't asked.

"What happened?" I asked.

"Dunno. Mum said he'd run off to join the Army, but I think he just went off with another woman meself. One minute he was there, the next he'd gone. Never saw him again. Me mum never talked about him, though me Aunty swore blind she saw him in the pub one Christmas."

"Do you have many memories of him, before he left?" I asked, wanting to delve into this unhappy man's unhappy childhood and hopefully find something positive in it.

"Not really," he murmured. "Except he shouted at mum a lot." Not the memory I was looking for.

"Did he take you out anywhere? Read you bedtime stories? Go to the park?" Surely, I thought, there must be some good memories he could fall back on.

He seemed to think for a while, and I tried to read his mind. There were some jumbled thoughts, nothing concrete. Then he said: "We used to go for drives, when I was little. Dad had a beat-up old car. Red, it was. We went to the fair, had an ice cream. Sometimes we'd stay out late, drive to the countryside and watch the sunset."

"That sounds nice," I said. "Did you have any brothers and sisters?"

"Not then. Mum had two more later on, to other men. Back then it was just me and me dad. Mum'd stay at home."

"It's important to children," I said, "that quality time alone with mum or dad. I expect you want to keep doing that with your boys, so they have happy memories of you when they grow up."

He grunted, and I suddenly heard a clear thought in his head. *Black ridge.* I had no idea what it meant, and couldn't, of course, ask him.

After that he became less and less responsive, and I concluded he'd decided I wasn't worth talking to anymore. He was looking sleepy, and as the end of his session neared, I tried – and failed – to get him to commit to see me once more.

"S'not worth the effort, Miss," he slurred. "I dunno why I came today…"

As he left, he turned and said: "You won't see me again."

He was wrong. Oh, so wrong.

Chapter 28

The following evening, Tuesday, Will came around to share a pizza and watch a film. It was a week since our trip out, and I was excited to see him again.

The pizza went down well, and we sat through a gripping thriller neither of us had watched before. It was pleasant, and homely, and I was feeling all kinds of happy when the doorbell went at about 9pm.

I wasn't expecting anyone. "It's probably Jehovah's Witnesses or something," I laughed as I went to answer the door.

"What, at this time of night?" he asked, not unreasonably.

Standing on the doorstep was Andrea, and I actually would have preferred the Jehovah's Witnesses.

She looked stern and unhappy, and a little scared. "Can I come in?" she asked.

I really wanted to say no, but courtesy made me beckon her inside. It was cold out, and a bit drizzly, and I was too polite to let even my sister stand out in that weather. Well, most of the time, anyway…

She started to walk towards the lounge, but I stopped her with a hand on her arm. I swear she actually flinched. "I've, er, got company," I said, and she stopped dead and turned to face me.

"I'll get straight to the point, Steph," she said in her best schoolmistress voice.

"Please do," I retorted.

She coughed as if she was clearing her throat. "Mum says you went to see her."

"Yes, I did. A week ago, I believe."

"Well, she's only just told us about your visit," said my sister, giving me a hard stare.

There was a pause. "And?" I asked.

"And she said… you were claiming to have some sort of supernatural powers." She laughed nervously.

Shit. I knew this was going to happen, I just **knew** it.

I laughed too, though I don't think it sounded convincing. "Excuse me?" I said.

130

Andrea was by this time fiddling with her right earlobe, which I knew was something she did when she was unsure or nervous. "Well, I know it sounds ridiculous, of course it does, but she sounded sure that's what you'd said. Said you'd demonstrated it to her. In fact she was really scared."

For a moment I couldn't think of anything to say, and then, to my shame, I did. "Maybe she's showing signs of dementia. I mean, she did forget to turn the gas off a few weeks ago, and there was the time…"

Andrea interrupted me: "Mum said you'd deny it. She also said you'd probably claim she had Alzheimer's or something."

"Well of course I'm going to deny it, aren't I?" I said. "Because it's not true!"

There was another pause, longer this time, and for a second I wondered what Will was making of all this – my house is only small; he'd be able to hear every word.

One of the problems I had with my sister – and of course there were many – was that she'd always been able to tell when I was lying. Nothing had changed. She looked me in the eye, and said: "Tell me you can't read minds, Steph."

"I can't read minds, Andrea. Christ, just saying that sounds ridiculous. D'you know how ridiculous that even is? Even your mate Jesus couldn't read minds, as far as I'm aware."

I didn't mean to goad her – I just wanted her to leave, and quickly – but of course she took my 'blaspheming' as a personal attack, and her face reddened. She was staring hard at me now, and I could hear her thoughts: *Tell me the truth, Stephanie.*

I remained silent. So did she.

After a moment I could bear it no more. "What do you want me to **say**, Andrea?" I blurted out.

"I want you to tell me the truth!" she shouted, and she sounded frustrated. Good. I really didn't want her to know my secret – I so wished I hadn't told my mother.

But then she played her trump card, and all was lost. Just as I was about to ask her to leave, and show her the door, her thoughts came clear and strong into my head: *Harry is in Hell now, Steph. His little body is being burnt for all eternity, and he's suffering eternal, unbearable agonies, AND IT'S ALL BECAUSE OF YOU!*

I turned towards her, and willed myself to stay silent, but my face betrayed me. I felt the colour draining from my cheeks, and my eyes widened.

"Get out," I said, my voice cold and hard.

She smiled at me then; a horrible, uncaring smile of victory. "I knew it," she hissed, "I just **knew** mum was telling the truth. I always knew there was something not right about you, sister."

"Get out," I repeated, and opened the door.

But instead of leaving she stepped half outside and waved to someone I couldn't see. A moment later, before I knew what was happening, her husband Tim and another man came up the path. I tried to shut the door on them, but Andrea was standing in the way, and they both came into the now packed hallway.

"It's true," Andrea said, sounding triumphant and excited. "She's possessed."

Confused, I just stood there staring. I had no idea who the second man was, until Andrea addressed him by name: "Reverend," she breathed, "what do we do? How can we help her?"

Of course, it was Reverend Cooper, Andrea's beloved vicar. What the hell was he doing here?

And then it dawned on me, and I turned and almost ran into the living room, where poor Will had been all this time, trying not to listen, I expect. He looked up from the sofa as I entered the room. "Is... everything OK, Steph?" he asked.

I must've looked scared, because he stood up and moved so he was in-between me and the door. "Who is it?" he asked.

Before I could answer, my sister, Reverend Cooper and Tim stormed in like three people on a mission, which I suppose they were. Andrea's eyes were blazing with what I surmised was religious fervour, Tim just looked confused, but the Reverend seemed determined to act. The three of them stopped in their tracks when they saw there was someone else in the room.

"What's going on? Who are you people?" asked Will, his voice strong and clear.

It was the vicar who came forward first. "I'm Reverend Jeremy Cooper, from All Saints' Parish Church. And you are?"

Will looked round at me. I said nothing, unsure what was going to happen and feeling increasingly powerless in my own home.

"I'm Doctor Will Reed," he said.

Tim spoke then. "Are you here on a professional basis? Has Stephanie been showing signs of psychosis, or something?" Andrea butted in before Will could answer: "He's her new boyfriend, apparently," she sneered. How she knew that I didn't know, but then was not the time to ask.

"Well, can someone please tell me what's going on?" asked Will, and the vicar took another step closer. "We're just going to take Stephanie to our church, where we can… help her," he said. His voice was excited, and I realised he'd probably never met anyone with real paranormal powers before. I expect he couldn't wait to get his holy hands on me.

"Oh no you fucking aren't," I said then, stepping out from behind Will. I was suddenly furious.

The Reverend blinked. "We need to address your little… problem," he said. "We need to cast the Devil out and make you pure again."

I laughed then, and it was a genuine laugh. I heard Andrea gasp, and the Reverend took a step backwards.

"I can assure you there's no fucking devil, demon or other evil entity hiding inside **me**, mate," I spat. "And you know why? Because there is **no such thing** – I hate to break it to you, you being a man of the cloth an' all, but it's all complete bullshit."

I was angry, and on a roll, and no-one was going to stop me. I went on: "Harry is not in Hell, thank you very much Andrea, he's nowhere – nowhere. His little life came to an abrupt and premature end, and that's the end of that. And no-one is going to persuade me otherwise. Hell, even if Jesus Christ himself came knocking on my door he'd have to do some fine convincing before I believed what he said. So don't think you pathetic trio can come into my house uninvited and try to tell me what's happening inside my head, because you can't.

"And as for my unexpected 'gift,' well, yes, I admit it, I can hear people's thoughts. I've been able to do it since Harry died, and I've no idea why. Maybe something broke in my head as well as my heart. Most of the time it's a pain in the arse – man, people think a load of shit – but sometimes, just sometimes, I can actually use it to help people, and maybe that's why it happened. I don't know. What I do know is that it's now a part of me, and anyone who tries to take it away, holy or otherwise, is going to have to fight me first."

Everyone was staring at me, shocked into silence. Even Will had wide eyes, but I didn't care.

"Now," I continued, while I still had the upper hand, "can you three please leave before I call the police, so Will and I can carry on our evening in peace."

The Reverend turned and headed uncertainly towards the door, obviously not prepared to handle confrontation, while Tim and Andrea stayed staring at me. "You... you really can read minds then?" Tim asked in a quiet voice.

"Yup," I said. "So next time you think I've got a better arse than your wife, I may just tell her." At this Andrea, her face puce, went after the vicar, her husband following close behind her. Just before they slammed the front door I heard him saying: "I never thought that, honest!" and I laughed hysterically.

When I'd stopped a few minutes later, tears streaming down my face from laughing so hard, I saw Will, still standing in the middle of the room, staring at me with a worried look on his face. I chuckled, wiped my eyes on my sleeve, then sat on the sofa, patting the seat next to me. He came and sat down, slowly, as if he might break something.

It took him a full five minutes to speak. I left him in silence until he felt able.

"So..." he said, eventually, "you can read minds."

"Yup," I said. "Why, is that a problem?"

"Er... well, not as such, it's just a bit... unusual, I suppose," he said. He sounded amused rather than shocked, and I was pleased. "And a little bit against all my medical training," he added.

"Yup," I repeated. "Tell me about it. I spent hours on the internet trying to find someone like me. Even Google failed. Actually, you get used to it after a while, and I block out most people most of the time anyway — it's just too annoying."

"I can imagine," said the good doctor, and then he turned to face me, and took both of my hands in his.

"What?" I said, looking into his lovely clear eyes. My heart started to beat faster.

"Can you read **my** mind, Steph?" he asked breathlessly.

"Do you want me to?" I asked, breathless myself.

"Uh-uh," he drawled, and I did: *Let's go to bed.*

How could I refuse?

Chapter 29

The next day was the day of my final session with Susan Shaw, formerly McDonough.

Will took me to work in his car, having stayed the night. He was on his way home to get a few hours' sleep before he started his afternoon shift. I waved as he drove away, feeling happier and more positive than I had done in a long time.

Will and I had talked for hours into the night, about nothing and everything, so I hadn't got much sleep and knew I'd have trouble staying awake later in the day, but I would be alright until then.

The first thing I did when I got into my office was check that day's appointments. Thankfully I only had three, the last one at 2pm, so I went into Gary's office and asked if I could take the rest of the day off. He said it was fine. "Anytime, as long as it's convenient," he said cheerily.

"Thanks Gary, you're a star," I said, and he smiled.

"Everything OK, Steph?" he asked. I smiled back at him. "Yes," I replied. "Fine and dandy."

My first session was a warring married couple who were supposed to be resolving their issues instead of divorcing. I'd seen them a few times before, and already come to the conclusion that nothing I said would help, but we went through the motions anyway – it was what I was paid to do. I'd tried reading their minds to find something underlying their disagreements, but came away with nothing – rarely, they both seemed to say exactly what they were thinking.

My second appointment was Susan Shaw, and I was actually looking forward to seeing her – after all, the last time had been really productive, she looked like she was heading for a brighter future, and I was pleased if I could end a client's sessions on a positive note.

But as soon as she walked into the room I knew something had changed.

Her eyes gave it away – they had dark shadows and a haunted look. She sat down gingerly, as if she'd hurt something, and at first refused to look at me.

I was instantly worried. "Susan?" I asked. "Is something wrong? Has something happened?"

She answered me by bursting into heart-wrenching sobs, and I did what I was never supposed to do – I left my desk, went round to her side and sat in the chair next to her. She turned to me and I hugged her – I could feel her tears wetting my top.

I held her like that – a bit awkwardly, to be fair – for a few minutes, before she regained control and pulled away. I passed her a tissue to blow her nose and wipe her eyes, and stayed where I was, thinking she'd be more likely to open up to me if I was on her side in more ways than one.

She sniffed a few times, and smiled weakly. "Sorry," she said.

"There's nothing to be sorry about," I told her. "Now, are you able to tell me what's wrong?"

She looked at me, and her eyes were scared as well as sad. "He's been threatening me," she said.

"Who?" I asked, although I was pretty sure I knew who she meant.

"Stu," she said. Her voice was shaking.

"What's he been saying?"

"It's not what he's been saying, it's what he's been texting," she explained, and she got her mobile phone out of her scruffy handbag. It was an old model. She held it out to me.

"You want to show me?" I asked, taking it from her.

"I want you to read them," she said, "and tell me what I should do."

"OK," I said, "but you'll have to get them up for me," and I handed her back the phone.

A minute later she'd found the texts, and put the mobile in my hand again. "Just press the arrow to see the others," she said.

The texts were difficult to read, and it took me a while, but I sat and scrolled through them all in silence:

Friday, 23:06: Ur dead 2 me now bitch
Saturday, 12:16: U r nothing. I hate u
Saturday, 12:17: hate
Saturday, 03:57: U will pay
Saturday, 04:07: I shd rape u but ur not worth th effrt

Sunday, 05:23: hdjbsa
Wednesday, 16:45: I gonna mak u pay fr wot u did
Wednesday, 16:48: Speak to me!!!!
Wednesday, 18:26: pls. I need to see th boys
Wednesday, 19:35: Bitch
Friday, 03:57: I want to tak the boys smwhr nice

He'd obviously then had a few days' break, because the next texts started again the day I had last seen him:

Monday, 12:37: Counciler sed u cant stop me seeing th boys I want to see them
Monday, 12:56: I no my rites
Monday, 13:02: Im getting a solicitr
Tuesday, 03:02: Let me see the boys or els ull pay

I handed the phone back to Susan and thought for a minute. I could hear her scared thoughts coming through in a jumbled way: *He'll hurt them, please God don't let him them me... the boys... need to stay safe...*

"Do you think he's serious about these threats?" I asked.

She sort of whimpered. "I know he is," she said.

"Why? What else happened, Susan?"

She sighed, and rolled up the right arm of her raincoat in answer. There was fresh bruising up her forearm, the red marks just turning to black and blue.

I winced. "What happened?" I asked.

She started crying again, but silently this time, and I passed her a fresh tissue. Once she'd blown her nose, she told me: "He met me after work, yesterday. I was walking to get the bus to go pick the boys up, and he stood in my way.

"He was drunk, and angry, and wouldn't listen to what I said. He... he pulled my arms, and hurt me, and pushed me to the floor. I couldn't make him listen. I tried..."

"I'm sure you did," I reassured her, "but he's not in the mood for listening at the moment."

She shook her head sadly. "He hurt me," she repeated, "and I'm scared..."

"Did you report it to the police?" I asked, knowing what the answer would be.

She shook her head again. "It'd only make it worse," she said.

I wasn't sure about that, but understood her reasons.

"OK," I said, "well, if you won't involve the police, you need to tell his social worker, so she can act accordingly." She looked at me, puzzled. "She might be able to have a quiet word with him," I explained, "to make him see that threatening you is not helping him regain contact with his children."

She nodded, and I went on: "Because that's all he wants, isn't it? To see his boys – and, to be fair, as long as he behaves himself he should be able to do that."

"After he's threatened me?" she asked.

"Well…" I said, "that was in response to you refusing to let him see them. Give him time to calm down, and realise the potential consequences of his actions, and I'm sure he'll apologise and start behaving appropriately again."

"But I shouldn't give in to threats, should I?"

"No… no, of course not. I just mean it's quite out of character for him to act like this; he's desperate to see his family, which is driving him to do things I'm sure he'll regret very soon."

She looked a little reassured, but was obviously still upset and worried. I didn't blame her. Last time I saw him, Stuart had not seemed at all repentant or reasonable. And him drinking all the time was obviously not helping.

My mind went back to those text threats, and an important thought came to me. "You always pick the boys up from school, don't you?" I asked.

"Yes, usually, why?" I frowned. "If I were you I'd tell the school that only you should pick them up." Her eyes widened, and I saw the thought enter her head, too. "Tell them not to let the boys go with anyone else, including their father."

"I will," she said, sounding scared again. "I'll tell them later."

We talked about other things then, me going around to my own chair after a while, and ended by summing up what she thought she'd got out of the sessions. It wasn't much – the aim had been to get the couple to agree on shared custody of their sons, and I had to admit I had totally failed in that regard.

Nevertheless, you can't win 'em all, as the saying goes, and I well knew that.

Before she left, I wished Susan good luck for the future, and – on the spur of the moment – gave her my personal business card, which had my mobile number on it, "in case you want to speak to me, day or night." I rarely gave that card out, but something told me Susan might need it.

I was not wrong – and it was far sooner than I had expected.

Chapter 30

I went straight home after my two o'clock appointment, which was with a new client who needed help with crippling anxiety. I was tired and just wanted to go to sleep for a couple of hours.

I let myself in and immediately Jess came bounding down the stairs to greet me, meowing loudly (I heard his primitive thoughts: *Food? Now?*) After giving in to his demands I made myself a cup of tea, grabbed a biscuit to dunk and then went to sit in the living room to relax.

I had drunk my tea and was just closing my eyes when my mobile rang. I immediately thought it would be Will – I had, of course, been thinking about him – but knew he would be at work by now.

It was a number I didn't recognise, and I expected it to be a cold call, so answered with the usual curt "hello?" I reserved for people from India trying to sell me something.

The voice on the other end of the phone was high, frantic and familiar. It was Susan.

"Miss Martin? I… I didn't know who to call. Please help me, he's got them, he's got them!"

"Susan?" I asked, "is that you? Calm down and speak slower. What's happened? Who's got who?" My heart sank, as I think it already knew the answer to this one.

I heard her struggling to breathe slower, and after a moment she said: "I got to the school a bit late, cos the bus was late, and they'd already gone. The kids. The teacher said their dad had come to pick 'em up." Oh shit on a brick, I thought.

"I tried ringin' him, but he won't answer. I don't know where they are!" She was almost screaming.

"OK," I said, trying to sound calmer than I felt. "I'll try ringing him, and then get back to you. Where are you now?"

"I'm still at the school. I told them he wasn't supposed to pick them up, but they didn't know, and I was so upset they let me come inside. The head said we should call the police, but I don't know if I should. Should I call the police?"

It took me a second to answer. A picture of Stuart, dishevelled and smelling of alcohol, entered my head, and I replied: "Yes. Get the head to call the police, and stay there. I'll ring you back in a minute."

She rang off, and I immediately called Gary – I didn't have Stuart's number, but it would be on file. Gary sounded concerned when I told him what I wanted, and why.

"Shit Steph," he said, "is he likely to do anything stupid?"

I thought again of his blank eyes, and shivered. "Maybe," I said, "although he loves the boys. They're his whole world."

There was a moment's silence. "That could be the problem," said Gary shortly.

Gary gave me the number, and I scribbled it down on a piece of paper. "Thanks," I said. "I'll let you know what happens."

A minute later I was listening to the ringing tone of Stuart's phone. He wasn't answering. I let it ring several times, then hung up and tried again. Still no answer. There was no voicemail option.

Shit shit shit... I decided to send him a text, just in case. My fingers were shaking as I pressed the keys, and it took me three goes to get it right. It said: Hi Stuart, it's Steph Martin from the counselling service. Please ring this number asap. Your wife is concerned about the boys. We don't want this to end badly. Call soon so we can work it out.

I thought it was as good a message as I could manage at that moment, so pressed send, not really expecting a reply. Then I phoned Susan back. She answered on the first ring.

"Hello?" She sounded scared.

"Hi, Susan, it's Steph – Miss Martin – again," I said.

"Did you get him? Are they OK?"

"I'm sorry, Susan, he's not answering my calls either, I'm afraid." I heard her sob. "I sent him a message – maybe he'll get back to me."

"He won't. He's going to take them away from me, I just know it," she said through her tears. I could hear a woman's voice, reassuring her, in the background. Presumably the head or a teacher.

"Has someone rung the police?" I asked, and she said they had. Well, I thought, there was very little else I could do. I suddenly felt very tired, and helpless, and in need of a cuddle. I could only imagine how poor Susan was feeling.

Actually, I knew exactly how she was feeling – most mothers would. When Harry had just turned two, he and I went to the swimming pool as a treat. He loved swimming, and I enjoyed taking him. We'd splash around in the shallow end for ages, while our fingers went wrinkly, until it was time to leave.

One day – I remember it as if it were yesterday – we were getting dry and changing back into our clothes in the cubicles, and Harry had been acting up, messing about, putting my dry clothes on the floor and demanding sweets before we went home. Typical 'terrible twos' behaviour.

Frustrated, angry at the way he was acting and uncomfortable because I was wet and cold, I put him outside the cubicle so I could get dressed in peace, telling him sternly to "stay there and don't move an inch." I could see his little feet, in their Batman trainers, under the cubicle door.

I turned away to pull my jeans up – just for a second – and when I turned back his feet had disappeared. I called him twice, but there was no answer, so I opened the cubicle door, despite being only half-dressed – and he'd gone. Just like that. Disappeared.

Frantic now, I rushed outside, calling his name, a towel wrapped round my naked top. Fear, dread, horror – every terrible emotion you can possibly think of, I felt it then. It only took me five minutes to find him, but I swear they were the longest five minutes of my life.

I found him in the pool foyer, ogling the vending machine sweets. There were plenty of people around him, but nobody seemed bothered a toddler was roaming the place on his own. I was furious – with him, with them, with myself. I'm ashamed to say I smacked him, hard, on his leg, in fright – the only time I ever smacked him. People stared, but I didn't care. They were lucky I didn't smack them, too.

Anyway… I knew how it felt when your child was missing. Not knowing where they were, or what was happening to them, was the worst feeling in the world. Well, almost the worst.

I told Susan to stay calm, to keep trying to contact Stuart until the police got there, and to let me know any updates, and then rang off. I knew she was being looked after, and there was nothing else I could do.

I stayed staring at the wall for hours.

Chapter 31

It was around two hours later – early evening, by this time – that I could bear the tension no longer. I **had** to know what was happening, so I rang Susan's number again.

Once more she answered on the first ring, as if she had the phone in her hand. She probably did.

"Hello?" Her voice sounded tired and small.

"Hi Susan, it's Steph again," I said, sounding quite shaky myself. "Any news?"

She suppressed a sob. "Well, the police brought me home, and they're here now," she said. "They say they're looking for them, but they can't class them as missing yet. They keep saying Stu's bound to bring them home soon, but I know he won't. His phone's just ringing out."

She went quiet, and I could sense her hopelessness. I felt some of it myself.

I didn't know what to say, but she went on: "I'd go out and look for them myself, but I don't know where to start. And the police've told me to stay here in case Stu brings them home."

I thought for a second. "Do you have any idea where he may have taken them? Any relatives, friends, special places?" I asked.

"The police keep asking me that, and I've told them – the only place they used to go was the park, which is just round the corner, and they've looked there already. There was nowhere else. We never had any money to go places."

"OK," I said. "OK... well, keep me posted, and try not to worry too much."

She rang off, and I sat thinking for a few minutes before dialling Will's number. I knew he was in work, and sure enough his mobile went straight to answerphone. I left a shaky message: "Hi, Will, it's me. I... can you ring me as soon as you get this please, it's a client – her little boys have been abducted by their father, and I'm worried he's going to do something daft... he's not the most reliable of fathers, and... well, I just need you. Please ring me."

A few minutes later I put on my coat and headed out of the door. I couldn't bear to stay there any longer, and I'd suddenly had an idea where Stuart McDonough may have gone.

....

I caught the bus from a bus stop a few streets away, and 20 minutes later was in New Berwick, the nearest seaside town.

It was a popular place for a day out, especially in the summer months – I used to take Harry all the time – and it was always busy as long as the weather wasn't wet. Today it had been dry, although overcast, and I thought Stuart might have brought the boys as a treat.

After all, I remembered one of his texts to Susan said he wanted to take them somewhere nice – and this was the closest and most obvious place to go with small children, especially if you were using public transport. There was a small fair, amusement arcades, plenty of restaurants and takeaways, a model village and a pleasant prom with gardens behind. You could have fun even if you didn't have much money.

I got off the bus with no idea what I was going to do. It was close to going dark – they could've been and gone by now, or they might never have been this way at all.

Still, it was better than waiting at home.

I headed into the first amusement arcade I came across, and went straight to the woman behind the counter where you go to change your money.

"Excuse me," I shouted above the loud music, "have you seen a man with two little boys this afternoon? The oldest boy would've been wearing a green school uniform, the youngest one not, and the man is scruffy, about 30, with long-ish brown hair?"

The woman looked at me blankly. "There's a lot of people come in here," she said dully.

"But can you remember anyone fitting that description?"

She shook her head. "Nah."

I tried the next arcade, and the next, and then went into a café, an ice cream shop and the fairground – although I guessed Stuart wouldn't have taken them there, because it was expensive to get in, and I knew he didn't have much cash.

Everywhere I went I drew blank looks, the odd concerned comment, but no sightings. It seemed hopeless, but I carried on. Something told me they **must** have come here.

It was starting to get dark now, and I was beginning to despair. Some of the shops would be closing soon – most of them stayed open late in the summer, but this was October, and there wasn't much business to be had after 6pm.

I spotted a hot dog stall on the promenade, close to the model village, and went over. There were two people in front of me, and I patiently waited my turn.

"Yes, love, what can I get you?" asked the man.

"I don't want anything to eat, sorry, but I'm trying to find a man who might've been here earlier with two little boys. The oldest would've been in a green school uniform, and the younger one in normal clothes. The man is about 30, quite scruffy, with long-ish brown hair. Have you seen them? It's important."

The man was shaking his head already, and looking behind me to where his real customers waited. "No, I don't think so, love," he said. "We get a lot of customers here, and I don't remember them all."

Disappointed yet again I thanked him, and half turned away, when a thought struck me like a hammer blow. Of course!

I turned back. "The man wouldn't have been wearing a coat," I said excitedly. "Just a t-shirt."

There was a look of recognition in the hot dog seller's eyes, and he nodded. "Oh yeah," he said. "Weird bloke, haunted look, looked bloody freezing, got his lads a hot dog each but none for himself. Yes, they were here this afternoon."

I sighed with relief. "Do you know what time?" I asked. The man shrugged, then replied: "Well, it was just after the kids came out of school, I suppose. We always get a lot of kids around that time."

"Thank you," I said. "One more question. Do you know which way they went?"

The man thought for a second. "No... but the youngest lad was asking for an ice cream, I remember that, because his dad was moaning about not having much money."

"Thank you," I said again, and walked away.

Well, at least I knew they'd been there. That was something, I thought.

I sat on a bench and rang Susan's mobile number. She didn't answer straight away, and I was starting to become worried when her voice said "hello?" This time she sounded like she was crying.

"Susan?" I said. "It's Steph again, any news?"

She sobbed, and I heard her mumble something. A second later a new voice came on the phone. It was calm and efficient.

"Hello? Miss Martin? It's Constable Marya Malik here."

"Oh," I said, "well, I'm in New Berwick, looking for the boys – I had a hunch they'd come this way – and I've just found out they were here earlier – I think just after Stuart picked them up from school. A hot dog seller saw them."

The policewoman paused before replying. "Well, that's good information, thank you – we'll send someone there as soon as we can. But I'm afraid they could be anywhere by now."

"Well, yeah," I said, "but they're on public transport, they can't have got that far in a couple of hours, and Stuart doesn't have much money…"

She stopped me mid-sentence. And what she said made my heart miss a beat and drained the colour from my face.

"They could be anywhere," she repeated, "because Mr McDonough took his room-mate's car without his consent. They could be a hundred miles away by now."

Chapter 32

"What? I'm sorry, I don't understand. His room-mate?"

Constable Malik's voice was concerned. "The man he was staying with, anyway – Raj Ahmed. Mr Ahmed returned home from work half an hour ago and discovered his car had gone – the keys had been in the house, as he doesn't use it for work. We're assuming Mr McDonough has taken it, because there was no sign of a break-in."

"I didn't know he could drive!" I blurted out, which seemed a stupid thing to say as soon as I said it.

"Yes, Mrs McDonough informs us he has had his licence for some years."

She then asked me for details of the hot-dog seller who had seen the children, which I gave her, and she obviously wrote down, before thanking me. As she was about to ring off, I asked her on the spur of the moment for details of the car they could be in.

She sounded surprised, but gave them to me anyway – an old red Ford Focus, whatever that was. I asked her for the registration number, but had nothing to write it down on. Five minutes later, after I had ended the call, all I could remember was the first half, but thought that would be good enough if I saw them: SA51.

I kept repeating the car description as I walked aimlessly around the town, undecided as to what to do next… red Ford Focus, SA51, red Ford Focus, SA51, red Ford…

My mobile rang, and I answered it. It was Will.

"You OK?" he asked.

I quickly told him where I was, and what I was doing. He sounded shocked, and a bit bemused. "Why are **you** looking for them? Shouldn't you let the police do that?" he asked, not unreasonably.

"Yes, of course," I said. "But, well… I don't know, I feel responsible somehow, as his counsellor, and thought I might be able to track down where he's gone."

Will didn't sound convinced. "You're just one person," he said, "and they've got plenty of officers out looking for them, I'm sure."

"Well, I'm the one who found out he'd been **here**," I said, a bit defensively. "Maybe, if I think hard enough, I'll remember something else he told me."

Will went quiet.

"Will?" I said.

"I can get off work early if you like," he said. "I can be there in… 40 minutes?"

I sighed with relief. I didn't want to be alone any longer. "Great," I said. "There's a big furniture store just as you come into town, by a roundabout – I'll meet you at the bus stop opposite."

He rang off, and on impulse I walked to the main car park, where I wandered around for half an hour searching for a red Ford Focus, SA51… of course I was pretty certain Stuart would've left long ago, and sure enough there was no sign of his stolen car. Anyway, it was now pretty much dark, and I could barely see what colour any of the cars were, never mind what make.

I walked out of the car park and headed to the bus stop with a heavy heart. Surely Stuart had told me something else? Something relevant? I could barely think… I was very tired, and emotional, and worried sick about those little boys I had never even met.

Will picked me up five minutes after I got to the stop. I was cold, but he had the heater on in the car and it was warm when I climbed in. He leant across and kissed me.

"Man you're freezing," he said. "Right, where to, Robin?"

I looked at him, puzzled. "Robin? Who are you, Batman?"

He frowned. "No… Robin, the woman in the Cormoran Strike novels… by JK Rowling?" I was still looking at him blankly. "The private investigator? No?"

I shook my head. "Sorry, I've not read them," I said. "Any good?"

"Not bad," he said, "though not as good as Harry Potter, of course."

"Well, of course," I said.

"So, where to?"

I had absolutely no idea where to look. I was tempted to ask him to take me home, to be honest, but he'd just come all this way and I thought we should at the very least make some sort of effort, so I said: "Just drive back towards home, for now – I'm wracking my brains trying to think of something he said, somewhere he may have mentioned, anything…"

"OK, you're the boss," said Will, and I smiled weakly at him.

We drove for a few minutes in silence before I filled him in with the details I hadn't mentioned yet, including the fact Stuart was now presumably in a stolen car.

"Oh great," he said. "So he could be anywhere."

"Yup."

More silence. "How did you get out of work so early?" I asked then, needing to change the subject.

Will chuckled. "Told them I was ill," he said.

"William!" I admonished, in mock horror. "That's terrible!"

He chuckled again. "I know," he said. "I never pull a sickie, but thought the situation warranted it."

We went silent again, with just the music coming from the car radio, which was tuned in to some local easy listening station. I suddenly reached over to the dashboard and turned it off.

"Sorry," I said, "I need to think."

I closed my eyes, and tried to remember the last time I had seen Stuart McDonough. I pictured him coming into the room, dripping wet from the rain, with dead eyes. I remembered he'd reeked of alcohol, and that he'd told me about his dad running off with another woman… and I'd tried to get him to recall happy memories of his father.

I opened my eyes and stared at the blackness outside. "He said his dad used to take him on drives when he was a kid," I said.

"OK," said Will. "Where to?"

I shook my head as if to clear the thoughts. Slowly, as if from a dream, Stuart's words came back to me. "To the countryside, to watch the sunset," I said.

"Oh, well, that's… helpful," said Will in a sarcastic tone. "That could be anywhere. Did he say anything else?"

"No… no, I don't think so…" I said, as we reached the edge of town.

And then, suddenly, it hit me. He hadn't **said** anything else, but he **had** thought something.

"Black ridge!" I shouted.

Will jumped. "Excuse me?"

"Black ridge! He was talking about his dad, and where they used to go, and I heard him thinking 'black ridge'. I didn't know what he meant. Have you heard of it? Maybe it's a place!"

Will was shaking his head. "No… it's not round here, at any rate," he said.

Damn. I had been certain that was a lead.

"Pull over!" I said then. Will obliged, stopping in the next bus stop.

"What?" he asked. He sounded almost as excited as I was.

"Does your phone have internet access?" I asked.

"Yes, why?"

"Google black ridge," I said. "My phone's awful…"

He pulled his phone out of his coat pocket and fiddled with it for a minute or two.

"Black ridge… are you sure that's what he said, I mean thought?"

"Yes, I'm certain."

Will was scrolling through the results. "Er, well, there's a black ridge mountain in New Zealand," he said, "but somehow I don't think they went there."

Damn, shit and double blast. It was the only lead I could come up with, and it looked like it was going to draw a blank.

Then Will stopped scrolling, and exclaimed: "Hold on a minute! Listen to this: 'Black Ridge: A popular tourist spot in North East England, featuring a climbing road with dramatic vistas of the local countryside. The summit has a café, car park and pleasant grass verges where you can take a picnic to enjoy the view.'

"Well," he continued, as I nearly jumped up and down in my seat with excitement, "that could just be the place, let's see…" he scrolled on a bit more "…it's by the coast, about… say an hour or so away. Do you think that could be it? D'you think that's where he's gone?"

I was wide-eyed with excitement. "Yes, I'm sure of it," I said.

"Well, let's go then," said Will, taking the handbrake off.

"Hang on," I said. "Should we ring the police?"

Will thought for a second. "Well, I doubt they'll act on it, but yes – will they still be with his wife?"

I was already ringing Susan's number. "I dunno, but it's worth a try." She answered on the first ring again, just as Will pulled out into the traffic.

"Susan," I said, "are the police still with you?"

"They left once my brother got here," she said, sounding disappointed – presumably that I didn't have anything positive to report.

"Oh," I said. "Any news?"

"No… nothing," she said, sniffing.

"OK, well, we may have a lead," I said, trying not to sound too excited, "so I'm going to ring the police and tell them."

She asked me what it was, and I simply said Stuart had talked about a place he used to drive to with his dad, which wasn't too far away.

I rang off after telling her to stay strong, and immediately called 999, asking for the police. I told them my story – I had to go through it twice before they understood what I was talking about – and they said they'd pass the information on to Constable Malik.

By the time I ended the call we were heading out of town again and driving towards the coast.

We were perhaps 20 minutes into the journey when my mobile went again. It was Susan, and she sounded hysterical. I could barely understand her, and had to ask her to slow down. When she finally spoke coherently what she said made my blood run cold.

"He's got them!" She was almost screaming. "He called me just now. He said I'd never see them again!"

Chapter 33

I tried to calm her down, but it was no use. She was absolutely distraught, and I could hardly blame her. After a minute or so of listening to her I asked her to put me on to her brother.

The man's voice sounded scared, but at least I could understand him. I asked if Stuart had said where he was, or what they were doing.

"He just said she'd never see them again, that was all," Susan's brother said. "She could hear the boys cryin' in the background, but he wouldn't let 'er speak to them. When she started askin' him questions he put the phone down."

Bastard, I thought, *he wants to torture her.* "Have you told the police?" I asked.

He said they had, but Susan had wanted to call me, too. I thanked him, and told him to keep me informed of any developments. "Keep Susan's phone free," I told him, "so he can get through if he rings back. And if he does, you go on the phone and try to keep him on it. He may talk to you rather than her."

I rang off, and told Will. He looked over at me, said nothing, and put his foot down on the accelerator. We sped through the night.

....

It was another 50 minutes before we started climbing Black Ridge. I'd never been there before – never even heard of it, despite living not too far away my whole life.

I couldn't see much in the dark – the street lights stopped at the foot of the hill, and there was very little other traffic on the road.

I was very scared – not just of what we might find at the top, but also in case we found nothing at all. What on earth would we do then?

And, if I'm honest, I was also terrified Will might drive off the side of the ridge – the road had a cliff on one side and what appeared to be a sheer drop on the other. I wasn't a good passenger at the best of times; that night I was sweating with fright. It was a good job it was dark, as I could see nothing at all over the cliff edge.

My ears popped as we climbed higher and higher, and I was beginning to think this hill went on for ever when we saw a sign up ahead which said 'Black Ridge Café 200 yards'.

A bit further on there was another one: Car Park 100 yards.

This had to be where they'd be – **if** they were here.

As we approached the car park Will slowed down, and my heart plummeted into my stomach. From the road we could see the whole of the parking area – it was only small, with the café on one side – and it was completely empty. A single light illuminated the whole of the space. The café itself was in darkness.

Will pulled in anyway, and stopped. We looked at each other.

"OK," said Will. "What do we do now?"

I shrugged, and got out of the car. Will followed. I walked to the back of the café, thinking there may be somewhere else to park, but there were no cars at all, just a few overflowing bins and the odd bit of litter blowing around in the cold wind. Up here the gentle breeze had turned into something approaching a howling gale.

I pulled my coat closer to my chest, and turned back to Will. "Shit," I said, "they're not here."

"I can see that, Sherlock," said the doctor, dryly. "So what do we do now? Any more ideas?"

I headed back to the car, desperately trying to think of something.

"Get back in, it's freezing," he said, and I did as he said. We sat there for a moment, staring at the darkness, and then Will turned the car round and headed back to the road.

"We may as well carry on up the hill and see if there's anywhere else to park," he said, pulling out into the empty road.

I said nothing, feeling bleak and empty. I was despairing of ever finding the boys, but the thought of going back home and waiting for something to happen was even worse.

It started to rain, and Will put the windscreen wipers on. All I could hear was the 'swoosh, swoosh' of the wipers and the patter of the rain as it got heavier. The car headlamps swooped around each corner we came to, but there was no other light – no passing cars, no street lights, no houses... it was like we were driving higher and higher into darkness.

Suddenly the blackness was broken by something shining up ahead to the left-hand side of the road. Will and I saw it at the same time. "A car!" I yelled.

It was a car, alright, with its headlights on, parked in a small layby on the cliff edge side of the road, where it widened into a flat area. Presumably this was a viewpoint, where in the daytime people would stop to take photos of the surrounding countryside, although of course at the moment all you could see was darkness.

Will pulled up a few feet away from the parked car, and immediately got out, leaving the engine running and the lights on. I followed, heart beating fast.

As I shut the car door I heard Will shout: "No! Oh God, no!" I turned, in time to see him run to the other car – my mind bleakly noticed it was red; I could see the colour shining in the beam of Will's headlights.

At first I was confused. If this was indeed Stuart and his sons, why was Will shouting? Surely talking was better?

But then I saw why he had reacted that way. The red car was pointing to the right, so its back end was facing us. In the glow of its rear headlights I could see something snaking from the back of the car to the front – something unusual, something you wouldn't normally associate with the sleek outline of a car.

At first my mind suggested it was a rope, and then I realised the truth. It was a hosepipe – and it was leading from the car's exhaust to the front window.

I knew what that meant – I had seen enough movies.

Stuart was trying to kill himself with carbon monoxide from the car's fumes – and take the boys with him.

Chapter 34

Starting to panic, I ran towards the car, where Will was already opening one of the back doors, but my legs seemed to turn to jelly and I nearly fell forwards.

My heart was pounding against my chest, and I suddenly felt very weak and fragile.

Thankfully, Will seemed to be coping better with the crisis. He quickly reached into the back seat and dragged one of the boys out by his arms, laying him on the cold hard ground. Without stopping to check the little body, he turned and opened the driver's door, then ran around to the other side of the car, where I could no longer see him.

I heard him shout over the noise of the wind and now driving rain: "Check to see if he's breathing! I'll get the other lad out."

By now I had reached the small, crumpled body of the first boy. He had a school uniform on, so I knew it was Lucas, the five-year-old. He was lying on his back, with his arms above his head and his legs at odd angles, just where Will had placed him a moment ago. He was already wet, his hair bedraggled over his eyes, which were closed.

At first I had no idea what to do – I was in shock, I suppose – but then I remembered what Will had just said. "Check to see if he's breathing," I mumbled to myself, and knelt down in the wet gravel beside the boy.

I bent over and put my right ear against his little chest. I couldn't feel or hear anything. Sitting up, I pressed my fingers onto his neck – I'd seen them do that in hospital dramas, to check for a pulse. Again, I couldn't feel anything. The little lad wasn't moving.

Frantic, I looked up, back to the car, where Will was hidden from view on the other side. All the car doors were now open, and I could see fumes billowing out from both sides. I couldn't see Stuart.

I looked back at the motionless body lying in front of me, and started to cry silent tears. "Will!" I shouted unsteadily, but I don't think he heard me. Presumably he was dealing with the other boy.

Trying to pull myself together, I decided if I couldn't feel Lucas breathing on the next try I'd have to start mouth-to-mouth. I'd seen it done on television, and once had a one-day first aid course at work, and presumably I was this lad's only chance, so I'd just have to get on with it.

This time I placed my hand gently on the lad's chest. There was no movement.

"OK, kid," I said, shakily, "you're on your own. Let's do this thing."

I tilted his head back by grasping his chin, like I knew you were supposed to, and opened his mouth. Then I pinched his nose and put my mouth over his, breathing out gently.

I can't tell you how many times I did this – not too many, thankfully – but I was just starting to think maybe I should be doing chest compressions as well, when the lad took a deep ragged breath and his eyes flickered.

"Oh, oh," I whimpered, sitting back on my heels and feeling a huge sense of relief wash over me. The rain was still pouring down, my tears mingling with it, but all I could hear for a moment was Lucas coughing himself back to life. His eyes flickered open, then shut again, but at least he was alive.

Wanting to know what was happening with his brother, I quickly got up and ran round to the far side of the car.

Will was kneeling alongside a small body – Ewan – on whom he was performing CPR. He looked up as I came into view, shaking his head to flick a stray strand of wet hair out of his eyes.

"Have you called an ambulance?" he asked, his voice strained from the effort of chest compressions. For a second I just stared at the little body lying in front of him on the gravel, then dug my phone out of my jeans pocket and shakily dialled 999. The screen was soon wet, but I managed to press the numbers.

"Ask for the police as well," said Will quickly.

I surprised myself with my calmness on the phone. I quickly told the operator who and where I was and what I needed, told them we had three casualties suffering from carbon monoxide poisoning, two of whom were children, and that one had just been given mouth-to-mouth while another was currently being given CPR.

They assured me they'd send help straight away, and I rang off.

Will was still pummelling the child's chest. There seemed to be no response. He looked up briefly. "The other lad, is he OK?"

I nodded. "Well," I said, "I gave him mouth-to-mouth and he's breathing. What should I do now?"

Will was panting heavily with the effort. "If he's still unconscious, put him in the recovery position, then go and check on the dad."

Shit, I'd almost forgotten about Stuart in the panic about the boys. I ran back to Lucas – he hadn't moved, and his eyes were still shut, but he seemed to be breathing OK; his chest was rising and falling. I carefully turned him over and put him in the recovery position. Presumably this was in case he was sick, so he wouldn't choke on his own vomit.

When he was settled, I looked over at the car Will had pulled him out of. There had been no movement from the driver's seat, and I couldn't see inside from where I was.

Dreading what I'd find, I stumbled over to the vehicle a few feet away on wobbly legs, and looked inside. Stuart was slumped over the steering wheel, one bare arm over his face.

Wanting to get him out, as there were still fumes inside (they were making me cough), I grabbed this arm and started pulling, hoping to drag him out. He'd be far too heavy to lift. His flesh was cold and wet from the rain.

I'd given him a few tugs – without moving him much, I have to admit – when he suddenly lifted his head and looked at me bleary-eyed. He started to cough violently.

"Stuart!" I shouted. "You have to get out! Come on!" And I pulled at his arm again. He tugged it away from me, and mumbled something I didn't catch.

"Come on! Your boys need you!" I shouted in his face, frantically trying to get him out. At least he was alive, although I had no idea how badly he'd been affected by the toxic fumes.

He pushed me away again, but I reached into the car and turned the engine off – at least no more gases would be escaping now. Fearing he may turn it back on, I took the key out of the ignition and threw it behind me.

The car had now gone quiet and dark, as the lights died. Stuart suddenly lunged at me and grabbed my arm. I don't know what he was trying to do, but I was scared, so I shouted at him to let go and pulled away. He swore at me in a drunken way, his voice slurred – whether this was from alcohol or the effects of the carbon monoxide I had no idea. I couldn't smell alcohol on him, but the engine fumes were overpowering everything anyway.

I stepped back, then turned to check on Lucas. I could only make out his outline, it was too dark to see anything else.

"Your lads are out of the car, Stuart," I said, but I don't know if he heard me.

"Fuck off!" he yelled. "Let me die!" And he fumbled at the ignition, presumably looking for the key.

"I can't let you do that," I said, internally begging the police and ambulance to arrive. Of course it had only been a couple of minutes since I rang them, and I knew they wouldn't exactly be just around the corner. This was a pretty remote place.

Deciding to leave Stuart to his own devices – he was alive, at any rate – I walked back to where Lucas lay, and bent down to check his pulse. This time when I pressed my fingers against his throat I could feel a faint but steady beat. His neck was freezing, and I took my coat off – sodden with rain though it was – and placed it over him to keep him a bit warmer.

Glancing back at the driver's door, and seeing Stuart was still in the car, I headed round to the other side to see Will again.

My heart missed a beat as I saw him still in the same position, still pounding the little boy's chest. He looked up as I approached, and even in the near dark I could see his eyes were sad. He shook his head gently, but carried on with the CPR nonetheless.

I stared at the little lad lying on the ground, and suppressed a sob. He was so little, just like Harry. I seemed to remember he was around the same age, and for a moment it was Harry lying there, all crumpled and bloody, his face white and waxy, his hair limp around his face, his eyes forever closed.

I turned away, the memories too much, the present just as bad, and staggered against the car door. My legs seemed to give way beneath me, and I nearly fell over into the dirt.

And then Will was shouting – I didn't hear what he said – and I turned and saw Stuart behind me, wild eyes staring at his little boy in the damp.

"No…no…" he was saying, and I started towards him without thinking. But before I reached him he turned and walked away, both hands grabbing at his unbrushed and sodden hair as if he was trying to pull it out.

As he disappeared into the darkness, I heard him saying "What have I done?" over and over.

I shouted at him, trying to make him stop: "Lucas is going to be fine! Lucas is OK!" But I don't know if he heard me or not. I looked back at Will, who seemed lost in his own personal nightmare, and then, reluctantly, followed after Stuart.

It was pitch black out of the light cast by Will's car headlamps, and I didn't know where I was going. I could hear Stuart stumbling up ahead, though, and could hear him mumbling to himself. He seemed to be crying.

I called after him: "Stuart! Please come back! The boys are going to be OK! It's alright – it'll all be alright, I promise!" Of course I was lying, on both accounts, but you say what you can to save someone, don't you?

The rain stopped as quickly as it started, and I could hear Stuart clearer. He was crying loudly, and I headed towards him across what was now grass. A few feet later I stopped short, as my legs hit what appeared to be a piece of wood a couple of feet above the floor. I looked down – it was a low fence across my path. I stepped over it, and gingerly walked forward.

It was really dark here – there was no moon shining a light, and the car headlamps were now far behind us. My eyes were just adjusting to the gloom – I could see a shape up ahead, which I assumed was Stuart. I heard him coughing, his lungs trying to expel the noxious fumes he'd inhaled.

"Stuart?" I called. "Let's go back to the boys, where we can see. It's dangerous here – there's a cliff edge, I think, not far away. Please come back with me. You could fall."

I stopped, not wanting to go any further for fear of coming across the precipice.

"Stuart?" I repeated.

"I used to come here with dad," he said then, making me jump. At least he was still there.

"Yes?" I asked.

"We'd watch the sun set over the hills…" he said in-between coughs, "and eat crisps… it was nice…" his voice was small and sad.

"Please come back with me," I said, trying to sound firm but shivering with the cold, my fleece now soaked through. "Your boys need you."

He laughed, then, and my heart sank. It was the laughter of a broken man. "They don't need me," he said. "No-one's ever needed me."

"Now that's not true," I started, but he interrupted me: "I tried to kill them," he said bleakly. "Do you think they'll ever love me again?"

I tried to think of a convincing reply, but drew a blank. "I…" was as far as I got, before I heard his thought come clear into my head: *They'll hate me forever.*

And then I heard him crying again, and his shape disappeared into the gloom.

"Stuart?" I called, and took a tentative step towards the way he'd gone. "Stuart?"

There was no reply, just the sound of the wind whistling around the rocks above and below us – and then I heard him screaming; a long, drawn-out yell of anguish and pain and despair as he threw himself over the sheer cliff.

I still don't know if his dying scream was in my ears or my head.

Whichever, it stayed there for a long time.

Chapter 35

They found his body about 150 feet below the viewpoint. They said he wouldn't have died immediately. I blamed – blame – myself; it's something I'll have to live with forever.

Lucas made a full recovery. I saw him much later on, and he was pink-cheeked and cheery enough, though there was a sadness behind his eyes I expected would never go away completely. At five, he was old enough to understand some of what had happened, but not all, thankfully, and I believed with the right amount of love and attention he would go on to lead a happy life.

Little Ewan never recovered consciousness, being declared dead as soon as they got him to hospital. Will never said so, but I think he knew it was hopeless to try to revive him at the scene – Ewan was already dead by the time we got to him. The smaller a body is, the quicker it succumbs to carbon monoxide poisoning.

It broke my heart that if I had just remembered Stuart's thought about Black Ridge sooner, we might have got there in time to save more than one of the trio.

I know it broke Will's heart for a time, too, although of course he didn't blame me – it was nobody's fault but Stuart's, and **he** had paid the ultimate price.

....

Late the following morning Will and I lay clutching each other in bed like little children – we were both too traumatised by our experience to go to work, and Will had insisted on staying with me instead of going home after an eventful night at the hospital and then the police station, where we had to give statements. It was after 4am when we'd eventually crawled into bed, and neither of us had slept much since.

I had sobbed myself dry, my head was pounding and my eyes were swollen. Will held me close, lost in his own misery but still trying to comfort me. I began to love him in that moment, I think.

Later that day, after a couple more hours' sleep, I woke to discover an empty and cold space in the bed next to me. Like in the days after

Harry died, I just wanted to sleep, to forget, but oblivion wouldn't come; so I struggled out of bed, put my dressing gown and slippers on and headed downstairs.

I didn't expect Will to be in the house – I thought he would have gone home – but there he was, in the kitchen, frying bacon and eggs. It smelled good, and my stomach made a hungry noise. It was a long time since I'd eaten, I realised.

Will looked up and smiled. His hair was untidy and his eyes sad, but his smile still made my heart leap.

"Fancy some breakfast?" he asked.

I glanced at the kitchen clock. It said 3.50. "Hardly breakfast... not even lunch," I said, "but yes, please."

We sat in companionable silence at the kitchen table eating bacon, eggs and toast and drinking large cups of coffee, until we both felt a bit more human.

Sipping my coffee, holding the mug in both hands, I looked into Will's dark eyes, blushed, and looked away.

"What?" he said, sounding half amused and half defensive.

"I...I just like you being here," I said uncertainly.

He smiled a half-smile. "Well, I like being here," he said. "Can't you tell?"

I must have looked puzzled, because he went on: "I mean, can't you read my mind?"

I'd half forgotten that he now knew my secret – in fact, that most of the town probably knew by now, if my sister had stuck to her normal moral standards and spread the word about her 'evil' and 'possessed' sister. For a moment I was silent, and I held my breath.

"It's OK, Steph," he said then, gently. "It's just a bit of a shock, that's all – it won't scare me away. Promise."

I breathed again. "I'm glad about that," I said. "because I don't want you to go away." I blushed again, and stared into space. Will was silent for a moment, and then got up and cleared the dishes away.

He was standing at the sink, with his back to me, when I heard him thinking: *That poor boy. I should've saved him. I should've saved him.*

Impulsively, I got up and hugged him from behind. My arms were tight around his waist, and I rested my head against his back.

"We can't save everyone," I whispered into his t-shirt.

He turned around and hugged me back. I never wanted to let him go again.

…………………………………………..

A couple of weeks later Jenny and I were sitting in the local pub, me sipping a colourful cocktail, she drinking lemonade, chatting quietly. The pub was nearly empty, which was just the way I liked it.

After much internal debating, and a bit of external debating with Will, I had decided not to tell her about my thought-reading – as far as I was concerned, the fewer people who knew the better.

Yes, she was my best friend, but I didn't want her – or anyone else, unless it was absolutely necessary – to treat me any differently, which they undoubtedly would if they knew I had the potential to listen to what they were thinking.

I hadn't seen or heard from my sister since that night she and her religious comrades had tried to drag me away to be exorcised, or lynched, or whatever it was they were going to do to me. My mother, too, had been strangely silent, although I had received a couple of texts from her. I was glad of their remoteness, to be honest – I would contact them when I felt the time was right, and not before. That may be never; I wasn't sure yet.

I had, of course, talked to Jenny about the incident with Stuart and the children. Explaining away the revelation of Black Ridge was easy – I just said Stuart had mentioned the place he and his dad went during our sessions, which was nearly true. The police also had to be told this lie, but it was simple enough to keep – after all, the only person who knew the truth for certain was now dead.

Jenny was her usual sympathetic self, and managed to cheer me up during our early evening meeting by making me laugh more than once.

But we kept returning, naturally, to my recent harrowing evening, and our meeting was necessarily sad.

It seemed strange to me that following Harry's death I had actively blocked out the event to the point of never talking about it to anyone – I truly believe my brain refused to acknowledge the details in order to protect my sanity – yet here I was, a mere couple of weeks after another traumatic event, discussing it with my friend in minute detail.

For reasons I cannot explain, this time I wanted – needed – to talk about it, as if putting what happened into words might make it trouble me less.

Of course we had also made the papers. Because there were children involved, it even made the national news.

This had added another, very unwelcome, dimension to the story – both Will and I had been pestered by journalists wanting interviews. We both issued statements to the press, to get them off our backs, but refused to talk to anyone. I believe a few journos from the less moral newspapers tried to dig up more information about both of us, but failed to get anyone to dish any dirt.

I avoided the newspapers and TV news for weeks afterwards, not wanting to see how we were being portrayed. According to Jenny, they kept referring to me as 'bereaved mum,' which I supposed was at least accurate.

Anyway, it died down after a couple of weeks – the story wasn't **that** interesting, apparently – and life returned to normal, as it usually does.

This trip out to see Jenny was my first 'public' outing since, and I kept looking around the pub to see if I could spot anyone snooping.

Jenny noticed. "There's no-one here, Steph," she said. "I promise – I had the FBI check it out before we came in."

"Oh ha, ha, very funny," I said. "It's not **you** being hounded by the press."

Jenny tutted. "Hardly hounded…"

"Three of them camped outside my house for two days straight!" I protested.

Jenny nodded. "I know, Steph, but it was a good story, you saving a life on a hunch…"

"A good story?" I almost shouted, and then instantly regretted it. "Sorry… it's just hard to see it as anything other than tragic when you're so close to it," I said, quieter this time.

Jenny put a hand on my arm, resting on the table. "I know," she said again. "It was – is – tragic. That poor boy…"

"I keep thinking that if I'd only tried harder with Stuart, I could've saved them."

Jenny squeezed my arm. "You did what you could. Without you, Lucas would be dead, too."

"I know, but that doesn't really make it any better," I said, tears springing to my eyes again.

"It will," said my friend. "With time, it will."

I'm not sure she was right, but as Will said, you can't save everyone – you just have to do what you can.

Chapter 36

Eight months later:

Will knocked on my study door before entering.

"Can I come in?" he asked.

"Of course," I said. "You can always come in, Will."

"Whatchoo doing?" he asked, sounding like a little boy.

I laughed. "Just finishing off my client notes," I said.

"Ooh, anything juicy?" he asked, and I laughed again.

"Do I ever ask you about **your** patients, Dr Reed?" I asked sternly, pretending to be cross.

He shook his head. "No, but then I can't read my patients' minds, can I?" he chuckled. "Yours are much more interesting."

"Oh, I don't know about that," I said. "Most of them have pretty dull thoughts, I'm sorry to say."

I got up from the chair and we both went downstairs. I said we both deserved a cup of tea and a piece of cake. It was Sunday, and Will had the day off.

Will was stirring the tea when he suddenly remembered something. "Susan McDonough – I mean Shaw – came into the walk-in yesterday," he said.

"Oh?" I asked. "She OK?"

Will nodded, and put the teabags into the bin. "Yeah, she seemed alright… well, not alright, but better, if you know what I mean." I nodded, knowing all too well what he meant, and he went on: "It was just a minor medical thing. She's got a new boyfriend, she was saying. Matthew, I think she said his name was."

"Oh good, she could do with a bit of happiness," I said sadly.

"She said he's really kind to her, and dotes on Lucas," Will went on.

"Good," I repeated.

We went into the living room with our cups and plates. Jess got up from his perch on the armchair to greet us at the door, and jumped onto Will's lap as soon as we sat down. He laughed.

"He loves you," I said.

"Well, who can blame him?"

I play-punched him on the arm, then took a big bite from my chocolate cake. "Mmm," I said appreciatively, "where did you get this one from? It tastes home-made."

Will sipped his hot tea. "The church fete," he said, and I looked at him sharply. "I popped in this morning on my way back to mum's with Mabel. Yeah, yeah, I know, but they do good cake," he went on. "And Jenny was there with the baby. She said to say hi." I smiled. Jenny's baby, Alice, was a total darling. I'd babysat a couple of times so far, and loved every minute.

A moment's silence later, he added, rather sheepishly: "I saw your sister there, too."

I put my cake down. I didn't seem to want it any more. "Oh? And what did the spawn of the devil have to say for herself this time?" I asked.

He laughed a little. "She said she wished you'd get in touch, as she was concerned about your welfare, and I said she had no need to be, as I was looking after you."

"I can look after myself perfectly well, thank you very much," I said seriously.

"Oh, well, I didn't mean..." said Will. I flapped a hand in his direction for him to go on. "Anyway, she said something about us living in sin, which I pretended I didn't hear, ha ha, and then said your mum was pleased you'd been to see her."

"Yeah, well," I said, "I felt I had to, really, with her not being well an' all."

"I know," said Will.

"It somehow felt... apt... time... to try and reconcile the family a bit."

"Well, I think you did good," said Will, and he leant over and kissed me on the cheek. His mouth was all crumby from the cake, but I didn't mind.

"Anyway," I started, "I'll probably be going back to see her again soon."

"Oh yes? Good," he said.

"Because I have something important to tell her, you see," I went on, nervous now.

Will put his empty plate down on the coffee table and looked at me. "Oh?" His face was serious, and I nearly laughed.

"Yes... as she's going to become a granny again, I thought I'd better let her know before she finds out from someone else." And I looked down at my stomach in a significant manner.

Will was staring at me, and I did laugh then. "You know, for a doctor you can be a bit slow sometimes," I said.

Realisation dawned in his eyes, and he smiled the biggest smile I've ever seen.

After we'd hugged, and kissed, and cried a little, then hugged some more – knocking an annoyed Jess off Will's knee in the process – I had a sudden, worrying thought:

What if the baby can read minds too?

I decided to keep that thought to myself – for the time being.

After all, it was very unlikely – wasn't it?

The End

Pam Bloom was born in Liverpool, England, and now lives in nearby Meols, Wirral, with her husband, teenage daughter, cat and many, many fish. This is her third novel. She hopes you enjoyed it – if you did, she would love you forever if you gave her a review, however short, on the Amazon website.

Also by Pam Bloom:
Books 1 and 2 of The Parallel Universe Adventures:
Whole New World[s]
Running

The third book in the Parallel Universe Adventures trilogy will be published as soon as Pam can get round to finishing it.

For more details go to Pam's website, www.pambloomauthor, where you can sign up to her email list, or look her up on Twitter @PambloomPam, Goodreads, Google+ or facebook. She will be pleased to connect with you.